WERDOUGH
INC.

Selina Rosen and Sherri Dean

Weirdough, Inc.
Selina Rosen & Sherri Dean
First Edition Copyright © Selina Rosen & Sherri Dean 2017

Published by Yard Dog Press at Create Space

Print Version ISBN 978-1-945941-05-4
Weirdough, Inc.
First Edition Copyright © Selina Rosen & Sherri Dean 2017

Yard Dog Press
710 W. Redbud Lane
Alma, AR 72921-7247

http://www.yarddogpress.com

Edited by Lynn Rosen
Cover art by Brad Foster

First Print Edition June 1, 2017
First EEdition 2017
Printed in the United States of America
0 9 8 7 6 5 4 3 2 1

DEDICATION

Selina says, "For everyone who never got that special toy they wanted when they were a kid... Count yourself lucky."

Sherri would like to thank her co-author, Selina Rosen, for putting her butt in a chair and making her write, and the BDG for keeping her alive on a daily basis.

CHAPTER ONE

In the Beginning

It was the newest toy that every kid had to have or they were going to cry and scream until they got it or die... just die!

David Pratt sat at his desk and looked out the window. It looked out not at trees and sky but over the floor of the toy factory. There had been a time when he'd had big goals and bigger dreams. With a doctorate in chemical biology he was sure he was going to set the world on fire—or maybe put it out. But the jobs he really wanted would hardly pay off his student loans, and the jobs he would have still felt fulfilled in that paid decent he couldn't get. David wound up taking the first job that offered him enough money that he didn't care that he wasn't doing anything he really cared about because at the time what he cared most about was making money. Since then on most days he felt like a glorified paper pusher, a sell-out.

Today he was also unemployed.

He looked at the papers laid out on the desk in front of him and didn't have to wonder why he had been sacked. The toy company had changed hands less than a year ago. They had retooled the entire shop and put all of their assets into a single new project letting everything else fall by the wayside. Now something was badly wrong with the new toy; he was sure of it. Yet he had developed the compound, and there was nothing at all in it that should be a problem. His recent experiments popped up no red flags. As he kept running tests and asking questions it became obvious Weirdough, Inc.— the new owners—didn't want to admit there was a problem, much less investigate it. He would neither stop his tests nor shut up about it, so now he had been fired. It appeared his services were no longer necessary. They thanked him very much and gave him a huge severance package then gave him till the end of the day to clear out; reminding him that everything except his personal items belonged to Weirdough, Inc.

David looked at the papers again and thought of the flash drive deep in his pocket. He wondered for the hundredth time that day how he was going to get it out without detection and then wondered if he should even try. The truth was he was glad he'd been fired; he was more than ready for a real change. His student loans were paid off long ago, and it was high time he did something he really cared about. Getting fired was going to force him to do what he hadn't been able to do—walk away from a steady, substantial check.

The problem with just forgetting about the problem was that right then what he most cared about was that they were shipping out thousands of cases of this crap daily, and somewhere between packing it here and some kid getting their hands on it, something that should be perfectly safe wasn't. Something simply wasn't right, and he wanted to be the one to expose them.

But part of him didn't want to take the risk. He could try to expose them and never get decent work again, or worse. There had been a time when David wouldn't have even hesitated to do what he thought was the right thing. Reality had knocked on his door in the guise of bills he needed to pay but couldn't, and he had buried his integrity and ethics in a deep drawer and covered it with the kind of money that paid those bills and got him a shiny sports car and a trophy wife. Which was sort of the definition of a sell out if anyone asked him, which they weren't.

David wondered what it said about him that he was sure the only reason he was hesitating to smuggle the flash drive out at all was because he didn't want to shove it up his ass and could think of no other way to get it out of the building without detection. Sure he was packing out his office, but they were sure to go through all his things. He'd have to go through a metal detector. Since Weirdough, Inc. took over, exiting the building had been only slightly less difficult than getting on a plane. The metal detector they had installed was a piece of shit and wasn't likely to detect the small amount of metal on the flash drive but... He was going to have to bag the mother fucker and stick it up his ass, which didn't appeal to him at all.

And why had that even occurred to him as a way to smuggle it out? His old college buddy, Scooter, had made big money keistering cocaine for the drug cartels back in the early nineties. Sure, he'd had the occasional discomfort, and once had a leaky bag that made him lose two weeks of his memory, but—at least in Scooter's mind—the cash reward made it worth the effort and he'd never been caught holding. Scooter had been a lazy, law-breaking stoner—but he knew how to get shit done without breaking a sweat.

David had always been the by-the-books guy, afraid to rock the boat. He was very uncomfortable with the concept of... being uncomfortable. Afraid of prison or getting fired. But this wasn't something that David could just ignore; something was happening to kids who played with a toy that he had developed. He might not yet know why, but there were now way too many cases for it to be a coincidence. He took a deep breath and picked through the drawer full of thumbtacks and rubber bands till he found an open bag of finger cots. He sighed as he removed one of the tiny rubber-looking things, held it up, sighed, stuck it into his pocket and headed for the men's room. Later he might feel brave, but in that moment he just felt sort of used and a little dirty.

David tried not to sweat as security went through the box containing his personal effects, but it was hard with the flash drive up his ass. He surely could have done without Hank from accounting's shout out of, "Just shit, Pratt! Don't make up a song about it!" as he was trying to "hide" it.

Now he was home (and still had it in his ass) because he had been checking his whole house to see if there were hidden cameras. He neither wanted to get caught with the flash drive nor be filmed removing it. The more he thought about how they had acted and how quickly they had fired him, the more paranoid he became. He turned the hot water on in his shower and let it steam everything up before he even tried to remove the flash drive, just to be on the safe side.

His anxiety made everything clinch up, and he had to work at it to remove his prize from his *tuchus*. He tried going into a meditative state, but that was hard when he was trying to pull contraband from his ass. The irony of the moment did not escape him; he hadn't wanted to stick the thing up his ass in the first place and now... it didn't want to come out. He tried thinking happy thoughts, but he hadn't had any in so long he found he was out of practice. Also it was hard to think happy thoughts when you had just been fired, you were pretty sure the company you had worked for was poisoning kids, and you had a flash drive stuck in your butt. In fact, all he could think about were all of the stories about guys showing up in the ER with gerbils and worse up their asses. How was he going to explain this to the team of people prodding at his ass with things that looked like tools from the alien autopsy from Roswell tape?

This thought made him just go in and grab it. Now he was washing his hands over and over and over again.

"Out, out damn spot," he muttered. He stared down at the finger cot in the trash can and thought *I will never see a condom the same way again.*

He stuck the flash drive in a box full of bandages then put it in the medicine cabinet. He shut the door and wiped away the steam, then looked into the mirror. *Now what?* It was a good question; he didn't have anything remotely resembling a plan.

He didn't think he looked like any kind of troublemaker, not even a horn blower. Nope, David had spent most of his adult life wondering who he was and what he should be doing, but he had never once considered it would include corporate espionage. Certainly he didn't look the part of a man who would steal company files by carrying them out in his bum, but then who really did?

His brown hair, beginning to grey at the temples, was the same style he'd always worn—not too short; not too long. It mostly covered his ears, it touched his collar in the back, and he constantly had to brush it out of his eyes. He had no scars or marks outside of a razor nick from a failed mustache-growing attempt to mar what he considered to be a mostly handsome if somewhat forgettable face.

David no longer had the trophy wife, so he didn't have to explain getting fired or anything else to anyone. Teresa had called him a lot of things when she was leaving, but perhaps the one that most stung was "boring". It didn't matter that he had been sick to death of her lying, spending-all-his-money ass and was just glad she was leaving; the things she said still hurt. David had been way over even trying to hide his disdain for her and everything she stood for long before she decided to "end things". Like the job, she wasn't what he wanted, just something to get in the way of him having what he did.

David was in good health, mostly fit with only a small spare tire. At six foot tall he had always considered himself an average man... but not anymore. Average guys didn't smuggle things out of a factory in their ass. Well at least not since the end of the Soviet Union.

If what he had done was a crime at all it wasn't a major one, and he was pretty sure they weren't likely to know what he did, much less bother to come after him. After all they fired him because he was trying to find out what was wrong with their main product, so they had to know if they had him arrested he was going to tell the authorities everything he knew—which admittedly wasn't a hell of a lot. The evidence certainly pointed to there being something wrong with the product, but he couldn't prove it with any of the tests he had run. He was perfectly safe, no one was coming after him and he certainly wasn't going to jail. At the worst he was going to have a case of hemorrhoids.

Of course knowing that and really thinking it were two different things. The paranoid part of his brain was sure he'd at least see the inside of a courtroom, if not a prison cell, if his "crime" was ever discovered. At the thought of prison he gave a quick unconscious tug at the seat of his boxers then shuffled out of the bathroom.

He continued a search of his house for an hour before admitting he was seriously neurotic to even think someone was watching him. After all he just wasn't that interesting. David calmed himself and tried to just think. Of course five minutes into his thinking process he decided maybe he wasn't being paranoid enough, got up and started searching the house again.

Finally exhausted and hungry he made a bowl of ramen soup and went back to his chair to eat relax and think. When he'd had a wife it had been steak and salad or fancy stuff he didn't know the name of—mostly cooked in some restaurant and carried home in bags. On most days he forgot why he had ever married Teresa then he would remember she was a good lay and go off to masturbate. Directly afterwards he'd feel a little dirty and then he would remember all the reasons why letting little Davy drive the human machine was a bad idea... you know, Teresa.

After he had eaten and seriously talked himself out of checking for bugs and or camera's again, he concentrated on the problem. *They wouldn't have fired me so quickly or stopped me investigating in the first place if there wasn't a real problem with that crap. It can't be a coincidence. A handful of people saying their children's personalities changed after they ate Weirdough is a coincidence; two-hundred-fifty complaints is not a coincidence. But I have checked that crap in my lab a dozen times and I can find nothing the least bit dangerous much less mind altering about it and the components I used to make it shouldn't be able to hold some kind of toxic mold spore. I have all the data on the flash drive, but what the hell do I do with it?*

David's eyes strayed to his computer where a steady stream of his personal photos played across the screen as his screen saver, and who was looking back at him? Aggy and Scooter. The three of them were standing in front of the drama building. They had all belonged to the drama club their first four years of college. Then Scooter had graduated—David still had no idea what his degree was in—and he and Aggy had to drop drama because grad school ate all their time. He earned his doctorate and shortly after that he and Aggy had gone their separate ways. It seemed like the distant past now. Though he couldn't say he didn't think of Aggy often, he hadn't actually spoken to her since he left Colorado Springs. He'd found her on Facebook a few years back and occasionally he might poke her, but if they communicated at all there it was in three to four word sentences. Neither of them ever seemed to know exactly what to say past *How are you?* and *I'm fine you?*

Scooter. David grinned. It had taken Scooter nearly as long to get a degree as it had for he and Aggy to get doctorates. If it wasn't for the drama class they'd all taken as an elective, he and Aggy never would have made friends with the likes of Scooter. They were nothing alike. Aggy and David wanted to be in school; they both worked hard to get and stay there and they had big plans for their futures. Scooter was mostly in college to deal and do drugs. He was there for the experience. David hadn't heard from Scooter since he left and when he tried he couldn't find him on the internet. Of course it didn't help that David had never known Scooter's real name.

David could ask Aggy if she knew where he was. Fact was that if it was bad, he'd rather not know. Scooter may have been a low life, but David had loved Scooter, and he didn't want to ruin his memories of him by learning he was in prison or dead—which was where David figured he was by now.

David knew where Aggy was, though; she hadn't sold out to corporate industry. No, she had taken a job as a professor. Aggy had worked for and received a huge grant for the science department and was pursuing her pet project, creating a bio-chemical fertilizer that wouldn't run off or pollute crop land or water ways. She hoped to bind animal waste and minerals together in such a way to make a plant food that in her words was so safe you could eat it. The project had a big scientific name, but Aggy just called it clean crap. She was head of bio-chemical sciences at the University of Colorado Springs—their alma mater—where she did two lectures twice a week.

As the picture on the screen faded to be replaced with somebody's kid—whose he couldn't remember and didn't care—David knew just what he needed to do. He would do it, too... as soon as he could figure out what to say to Aggy.

Aggy rubbed at her tired eyes. "Old age sucks," she mumbled to herself. She remembered a time when being in the lab till three in the morning was no big deal. She looked at the clock and sighed. *Please tell me that says three and not nine. I just can't be ready to pass out at nine.*

She immediately got mad at her lab assistants. *Stupid-assed, wet-behind-the-ears kids party all the damn time, I know they aren't studying. What do they think that I was born yesterday? If I was born yesterday I'd still shit yellow and I wouldn't have crow's feet! Nobody has any work ethic anymore and... Dammit, I just turned into my grandmother... When I was in grad school I didn't fart around partying all the time, I put my nose to the grindstone. I would stay in the lab all night and...*

Her thoughts took her unwillingly to a place and time when in minutes her life had gone from light to dark. She and everything and everyone around her had changed in an instant. In that moment Aggy admitted she didn't make her interns stay when they wanted to go because she didn't want to be responsible if something happened to them.

She refused to live in fear; she had lived. Aggy didn't worry about her own safety because ever since she had been attacked on campus all those years ago she packed heat.

She would have been the attacker's fourth rape victim however she fought back and wound up falling down a flight of steps breaking her arm and collar bone, bruising her spleen, and giving herself a concussion. The perp had been caught because she'd drug him down the stairs with her. He'd badly broken a leg and he couldn't get away from campus security. On good days she reminded herself that she had stopped him. He was still in jail; she was healed. On bad days she admitted only her bones and guts were healed and that she would always carry a piece of that night with her.

The attack, far from making her more timid, had left her the kind of person who often waded in where wise men wouldn't tread. She said what she thought and thought what she said. All these years later she still couldn't tell you whether that was a good or bad thing.

She didn't have to stay; she could just call it a night and go home. Being in charge had its perks. There was a rum and coke at home calling her name, but not as loudly as her need to finish this set of tests. Why? Did anyone care about this project except her? If she was successful it would be an amazing boom to the environment. It would create more crops, cause no damage, feed lots of people... and she was damn close. She had already created a couple of better-than-everything-else fertilizers that were already on the market, but now she felt like she was just one pitch away from a home run.

She should have been ecstatic, but she couldn't for even a minute convince herself that anyone—even her interns—gave a diddly damn about her pet project. The university appreciated her as a professor, but mostly as a grant writer. The government gave her grants only because it let them then pretend that they gave a damn about the environment. There were a few farmers who appreciated her products, and who would appreciate it even more if she could actually do what she'd been trying to do for twenty years. But there wasn't going to be a parade with people throwing flowers at her feet because she had managed to create clean shit.

It shouldn't matter. She should be doing it just because it was the right thing to do because it was going to help save the world.

Somedays it was hard to even pretend to be selfless.

Right then she just needed a huge round of applause for even trying to do what she was doing, because without appreciation how was she supposed to know what she was doing was even important? If she succeeded was it going to be like the fertilizers she had already created where only a handful of farms used it because it was more expensive than chemical fertilizers that washed off and polluted everything from streams to the oceans. At the end of the day most people were too damn selfish to care about something they were all too ignorant to understand would go a long way towards saving the whole fucking world. And maybe that was the real problem; that she couldn't be happy with an end product that was most of the way there. It had to be earth changing or she wasn't ever going to be happy with it.

Even if I create something that's everything I want it to be, if it's expensive to make no one will manufacture it and even if they did and it pushed everything else off the market no one's going to say a hundred years from now, "Without Agatha Crystal's Clean Crap we all would have gone the way of the dodo bird." And if I can really do it, if I really can and if they use it and it does everything I say it can do... why do I need credit? Because I'm broken, damaged and beyond repair.

She pushed away from her microscope with a sigh. She could no longer even tell what she was looking at. For a minute she wondered if SHE cared anymore. Maybe she should have taken Scooter up on his offer to go in partners on his medical marijuana store. *Lots of money, no headaches, and lots of people saying you changed their lives for the better. All stoned out of their heads of course, but at least they'd say it.*

The problem was she didn't really believe in the benefits of grass, and she had never smoked the crap. In college she had used way too much hair spray and was always afraid her whole head would go up in flames if she so much as lit a match. Thank God grunge came into fashion and... well she'd worn her long hair straight and down and the same baggy jeans, t-shirts and flannel shirts ever since. She just threw a lab coat on over it if she was lecturing or working and pretended like she looked professional. Oh she got dressed up when she thought she needed to, but certainly she didn't feel like work was one of those places.

People who went home early had a personal life. Still she was tired and it would take her a half an hour just to get the lab to a point where she could leave. She finished making her notes, admitted this batch didn't have as much promise as she had thought. *Maybe this is just a huge waste of time. I mean clean crap. It's an oxymoron. Bio-Chemicals are still chemicals and maybe at the end of the day the best thing to grow crops in is just plain good ole shit. But shit runs into rivers and streams and makes toxic algae bloom and the chemical fertilizers we have now leave toxic residue. If I can perfect a cleaner fertilizer... it will be my legacy. Until some big company slaps their name on it.*

It didn't matter; she would know. She went back to work. Aggy always went back to work.

This time when she looked up at the clock it was nearly midnight and she didn't feel quite like an old lady packing it in for the night. Besides, she had finished what she wanted to accomplish which meant she would probably be able to sleep when she got home.

She hurried to get things cleaned up and put away properly. She hung up her lab coat and thought about her old friend rum and coke waiting patiently for her to return home. It hadn't been a bad day's work; she really was getting close. Of course after all these years she ought to be. The fact someone wasn't up her ass on a regular basis asking where she was proved, at least to her, that they didn't give a damn whether she actually succeeded or not. She had already produced product that was making them all money.

She was about to flip the lights off and leave when the door swung open.

David didn't know what kind of welcome he was expecting, but this wasn't it.

Aggy stood there both hands on the grip of the biggest gun he had ever seen. She yelled, "You so much as move and I will shoot you dead in your tracks, you son of a bitch!"

CHAPTER TWO

Hello Again

"Damn, Aggy I didn't know you were still this mad," David said as he raised his hands palm open over his head.

"What?"

"It's me, David... David Pratt."

"Well fuck, David." She lowered the gun. "You might have tried knocking on the door. Or maybe a phone call to tell me you were coming. You remember a phone? It's that thing that you call people on when you want to talk to them. Wait, oh now I'm remembering! You didn't know how to use a phone way back then, and I doubt you do now."

David wondered if she was going to lower her gun any time soon. She finally did and even put it back in the bag he assumed it had come from. David lowered his hands and chuckled a little.

"Damn Aggy you're fast."

"I am, and you're damn lucky you didn't end up with a bullet in your brain. How the hell did you get past campus security?"

"I may have gone into the corporate world, but I'm still a scientist, an alumni. I showed him my card, explained that we were old friends from the same class, and he waved his wand over me to make sure I was clean and let me go."

"I think calling us old friends is pushing it a little." But she grinned when she said it. "What the hell are you doing here?"

It was a good question. They hadn't parted on the best of terms—they weren't really bad, but they certainly weren't good—and except for brief, uncomfortable not-quite-conversations on Facebook they hadn't spoken much less seen each other since he finished school and went off to seek his fortune.

They met somewhere in the middle and embraced. At first he could feel the tension as she embraced him, but then as he loosened up so did she and it became a real hug, one that showed him that there were still at least the bonds of friendship between them... You know, like she didn't really want to shoot him.

As they parted he still chose his words carefully. "You look well. You haven't really changed at all."

She laughed, a sound that he remembered fondly and said, "You lie! I didn't used to have this spare tire or all this grey in my hair, and I don't draw these lines on my face anymore." A reference no doubt to when they had both been active in the drama department.

"You still look good to me. I mean, hey, I also have the spare tire and the grey hair and the lines I didn't draw on. I think that comes with the territory."

"Ah, but I didn't feed you some bullshit about how you look the same as you did nearly twenty years ago." She smiled. She always did have a great smile. "So what the hell are you doing in town in the dead middle of the night?"

David took a deep breath then let it out. "Well..." He took another deep breath and let it out.

"For the love of God, David, I'd like to get some sleep tonight. Just spit it out."

"Well I..."

"You what... I'm not giving you a fucking kidney."

For some reason that made David relax. After all he wasn't asking for a kidney. "I have a problem and I can't think of anyone but you that can help me with it."

"If you are coming to me you must be out of options."

"Precisely."

She had started laughing and before David knew it he was, too.

"I knew you were a little uptight, but I never pictured you with an actual 'stick' up your ass!" She downed the rest of her drink and got up to fix another. She waved the bottle of rum in his direction, and when he nodded yes poured two more drinks, heavy on the rum.

David cleared his throat. "Yeah, I have no idea how much trouble I could be in legal or otherwise for taking it. I want your help, but I don't want you to get in any trouble and seriously I have no idea how much crap it might be."

"You always were the world's biggest weenie. It's your flash drive, right? And I doubt they'd want it back if they knew where it had been." Aggy laughed. "Let me tell you something, Dave, I don't really give a diddly shit about a little trouble and taking down a bunch of corporate goons... Well that may be just what I need to cheer me up right now."

When David woke up in the morning on Aggy's couch the TV was blaring and Aggy was basically sitting ON his feet watching TV, a coffee cup clutched in her hands. "That clown has got to be the creepiest thing I have ever seen."

David pulled his feet out from under Aggy's ass. "Yes, yes he is except wait... the worst thing is that the product he is selling is screwing up kid's brains made only creepier by the fact that kids adore him."

"Dude I think the marketing department must have been on crack." Aggy said. She spilt some coffee on the floor and just ignored it. From the look of the floor it wasn't the first time.

The huge clown on the TV was a technicolor nightmare. Pork Chop the clown's bloated belly ballooned out over pants that enveloped his legs in bright stripes and plaids. His shirt, equal parts baby-shit yellow and puke green, were topped with a purple ruffle that set off his pasty white face. A grinning red maw that appeared to have been drawn with an unsteady hand hung below a bulbous, equally-red nose. When the clown grinned a mouthful of yellowed teeth made their appearance, the same hue as his filmy eyes. A rainbow wig hung precariously on his head, held in place by a black porkpie hat and its cheap elastic band.

"Hey there kids," Pork Chop the clown said in a voice that sounded just like the Stewart character from MAD TV. "We all love Weirdough; it's the best! We can do anything with it make rockets to go to the moon or submarines to go deep under the sea, but we can never, never leave our Weirdough out of its air-tight container. It must go home. Weirdough doesn't mind if you play with it but like all good girls and boys after playing it just wants to go home."

The commercial ended and Aggy turned to him. "What happens if you leave Weirdough out of the container?"

"Nothing really it gets a little sticky. If you left it out long enough it would eventually get hard and turn to dust, but that would take a long-assed time. Of course even then if you wet it, it comes right back so... I kind of don't get the whole 'keep it in the container' thing. I think it may just be a marketing point. You know, parents think the clown is teaching their kids to put their things away."

"I've read through the files. I can see why no one's really paying attention. I mean it's not every day you get complaints from parents that their children are better behaved, are making better grades, do what they're told..."

"I know, right? At first I thought it was some joke but when they just kept coming in and I started to find all the... Little Johnnie doesn't hug us or engage with us, is distant and cold... killed the family pet. That's the big, red flag. Three of those kids killed the family pet. It's almost like they eat the Weirdough and it gives them a form of autism."

"We don't know that they are eating the stuff."

"The parents all seem to think they did and... well, they can't find it and like you said the stuff isn't going to go away anytime soon."

"But you know how kids are, Aggy..."

"No I really don't," Aggy said with a grin. "You have a houseful of the little buggers?"

"No but my brother and sisters do. They lose shit all the damn time. My brother said it's like they have a black hole into which the kids throw things that are then never found again till they are usually stuck to something you once loved."

"So you are saying it might still be in the house? That they didn't eat it."

"No I'm saying we don't know."

"So dumb ass, if they didn't eat it, if it is exactly what you say it is, then how the hell could it possibly make them sick?"

"Well... did you see how the shit glows in the ad?"

"Yes."

"Well the stuff I made doesn't glow and the stuff I've been testing doesn't glow. In fact as far as I know it's not glowing when it leaves the factory. They've never let me test the stuff that glows. They have to be adding it at another location, but why the hell would they do that? I asked the boss about it and he told me it was a naturally-occurring bioluminescent they gave me that to test and I tested it with the Weirdough components. It still seemed safe enough to eat, but there has to be some reason they add it later and why they fired me so quickly when I started asking question. They are hiding something."

"Hey, Einstein, did it ever dawn on you to go to the store

and just buy some containers of the shit?"

David grinned. "Hello I was working for them. Why would I spend my own money?"

Aggy called in to the university switchboard. She pressed the appropriate numbers to get through and waited while it rang.

"Lab, can I help you?" a bored, detached, almost-human voice drawled.

Aggy sighed. Why did no one under forty know how to answer a phone? No matter how hung over the little dumbass was, she should just fake happy the way Aggy did. "Marie? This is Doctor Crystal."

"Oh! Oh, hello Doctor Crystal!" Marie said, suddenly coming to life.

"I need you to run an errand for me. Take Denton or one of the other techs with you. Get me a couple of cases of Weirdough and bring it back to the lab."

"Weirdough? Like the stuff the creepy clown sells?"

"Yes. I need at least two cases."

"You realize it's only six weeks till Christmas and everybody's kid is screaming for that shit. We may have to go to more than one store to get that much."

"Do what you have to. Go to another city. I don't care if you have to go to a dozen stores. I need enough for a double-blind test study and I need it now. And don't tell anyone why you're buying so much. Tell them you're buying it for an orphanage, Merry Christmas and all that good crap."

There was silence for a few seconds. "But... why are we buying it? Why are we studying it? And should I take the money out of petty cash?"

"Because I said to that's why. Yes take the money out of petty cash."

"You just can't get good help these days." When she hung up she looked over at David, rubbed her hands together cackled and said, "And so it begins. Operation bring down the clown."

"Seriously, Aggy, you could get in a lot of trouble..."

"For what? Buying toys for orphans? Seriously, David, quit being such a wanker! What's the worst that can happen, a mad clown shows up and slings silly putty at us?"

"Well that for starters."

The minute Aggy opened the little air-tight container and they could see the glowing goo David who was standing looking over her shoulder said, "The crap they gave me did not make the putty glow like that even when I added twice what they told me they used."

"Interesting," Aggy said, and dumped it out on the table. She picked up a rubber mallet and hit it. David jumped.

"Why did you do that?"

"Because it said on one of the commercials that if you hit it, it would shatter but it really only just cracked... but look it's coming back together. That's pretty cool."

"I thought you were going to test it not play with it."

"You always were a kill joy. You test your way; I'll test mine."

One of the first tests they did proved that there was none of the bioluminescent chemical they had given David to test present. After hours of looking for and not finding a single chemical present that would cause the glowing, David and Aggy turned to each other and at the same time said, "I have no idea why it's glowing."

"It shouldn't be glowing at all," Denton said, looking over both of their shoulders at the computer screen. He was a nice kid, tall and thin as a rail with a shock of too-black-to-be-real hair and blue-blue eyes, who was really good at telling you what you already knew.

"Thank you, Captain Obvious," Aggy muttered.

"That's pretty fucked up," Denton said.

Aggy sighed. "Yes, yes it is."

David smiled at her and said in a whisper, "He's cute but kind of clueless."

"I picked him because he reminded me of you."

Marie, who had been carefully reading the smuggled data said, "This whole thing is pretty messed up. Do we have enough to call for a recall of the toy?"

"She is also pretty but mostly stupid," Aggy whispered in David's ear.

David started to say something and Aggy snarled at him, "So nothing like me. That's what you were going to say, right?"

"Precisely."

"We are talking about millions of dollars. To stop them we have to have hard scientific evidence that there is a link between Weirdough and Junior killing the family cat to see what's on the inside. So far all we have proven is that... there is no reason at all for this shit to glow.

CHAPTER THREE

Why Does It Glow?

David was sleeping on Aggy's couch again. It was uncomfortable, too short, lumpy and only clean if you didn't breathe too deeply and squinted when you looked at it. Aggy's home was modest, cluttered and not filthy but certainly it wasn't what he—or anyone else—considered clean. There was a slight scent of cat urine and funk that he didn't want to think about... mostly because he had yet to see a cat.

There were books stacked in piles everywhere; there were a few shelves they were mostly empty. No doubt because having the books in the shelves meant they weren't within reach of the places she obviously sat. There was a strange order to the stacks; each book seemed to be there for a reason. David had a feeling that if he asked Aggy for any book on any stack she could go right to its stack and pull the book out.

He'd like to think he was having trouble sleeping because as a bed the couch made a wonderful medieval torture device. Or because he had no job, or the reason he had no job. David would love to think that the reason sleep eluded him was that he was worried sick about all those kids exposed to a product he helped to create. He'd even settle for believing he was this angst-filled and restless because two scientists and two lab assistants spent a whole day and most of a night looking for a reason for a kid's toy to glow and never found one.

However he knew exactly why he couldn't sleep because he couldn't stop thinking about it. *I want to talk to her, really talk to her ask her what happened and why but I just can't bring myself to ask the hard questions. Nothing was ever the same after Aggy was attacked. We went from having a good, healthy relationship to having nothing at all in a matter of months. I'd rather lie here and toss and turn playing "name that smell" than start a conversation with Aggy about how our relationship ended and why because I still don't know.*

How many times had he relived that night?

They were working late in the lab. The professor—whose

job Aggy now had—had them working late, running tests. David was tired; he had hit a wall. Aggy wanted to do one more test... Aggy always wanted to do one more test, but she could tell David wasn't feeling it. "Go on home I'll be there in a few minutes."

He went home. He had barely taken his shoes off and sat down to eat a bowl of ramen when the phone rang, and nothing was ever the same again. She was angry and distant, cold even. He was guilty and confused. He had no idea what to do or say to make her feel better and everything he did just seemed to piss her off or make her feel worse. In the end they didn't so much break up as they cracked apart like the Weirdough did when she hit it with the hammer. There hadn't been any screaming, no throwing or breaking things, like the scientists they were they just sort of decided that early testing had proven they shouldn't be together till they weren't anymore.

And the truth is I have never cared about, much less loved, anyone the way I did Aggy and I don't think I ever will.

So he lay there tossing and turning because he didn't have the balls—even twenty years later—to walk into her room and ask what the hell happened to them.

He sniffled, not that he was crying—because that was for pussies—but because his sinuses were acting up. He'd always been slightly allergic to cats... of course he still hadn't seen a cat.

Why does it glow? Aggy tossed and turned. Scientists hated it when something that shouldn't be was. "There is nothing in it. Not a single chemical or compound that should make that shit glow." She realized she had spoken allowed and cringed. she lived alone and she often talked to herself. She'd had a cat once but it was mostly just there until it wasn't. She'd looked and looked but he wasn't in the house or in her small yard. *Ornery cuss, I wonder what ever happened to him?* Except for the cat, the only time she hadn't lived alone since she had left her mother's house was when she had lived with David. How weird was it that he was sleeping on her couch now, that after twenty years he just showed up hauling a problem with him. *David coming here now is even weirder than the fact that crap glows.*

Why? Because not three days ago she had picked up the

phone and almost called him. Her shrink said she thought the twenty-year-old unfinished business between them was keeping Aggy from moving forward. So after her session she had opened her Facebook page and scrolled through her messages till she found the one where he had given her his cell phone number. Her shrink said the fact David had found her on Facebook, friended her, and then had given her his number meant he was looking for closure, too.

She had every intention of calling. She even mostly dialed the number. Then she remembered two things. First, she was stupid even thinking of trying to find closure by talking to a man who handled conflict by walking around it and then running away as fast as he could. Second, Aggy only went to that shrink at all because the dean and the board of trusties insisted she go.

Aggy had lost her cool and smacked one of her interns in the face with a rubber glove covered in liquid plant food—so in laymen terms, wet shit. Whining candy-ass that he was he had turned her in for abusive behavior; he claimed it was a hostile working environment. Aggy carefully explained that the guy was being a total wanker, and that it was his fault there was fertilizer on her glove in the first place because if he wasn't such a klutz that he managed to spill an entire tray of samples she wouldn't have had to spend even a second trying to keep them separate before giving up, dumping the whole tray into the sink, and slapping the moron in the face.

Realizing the truth wasn't helping her case any, Aggy changed her story explaining how it was really just an accident and a misunderstanding. Aggy dug deep and pulled up a big dollop of her acting ability. "I was taking my glove off; it got stuck and the next thing I knew..." She did a performance deserving of an Oscar, but they didn't buy it. To keep her job and avoid a lawsuit Aggy she had to go to the shrink to deal with her anger issues.

She also got a new intern.

Now David was sleeping on her couch. He obviously had no more idea how to find them both closure after twenty years than she did. There was still something hanging between them like a question that gets asked that you know the answer to but don't dare say because you know the other person isn't ready to hear it. The problem was she wasn't sure that twenty years later either of them was any better equipped to deal with it than they had been two decades ago.

It was ancient history, but with him in the next room it didn't seem that way at all. And all the "what if" questions that normally popped up for a minute and then went right back where they belonged just kept talking in her head till they near drown everything else out including her desire to sleep.

She shook her head and tried turning over to get more comfortable which she wasn't. The real problem was she couldn't shut her brain off, and how could she? David was in her house and there was crap that shouldn't be glowing in their little plastic containers in her lab.

In the car on the way to the lab David found himself wondering why on earth he had let Aggy talk him in to taking her car and then into letting her drive. He had been reminded as his fingernails dug into the dashboard that Aggy drove way too fast for someone who wasn't really watching where they were going—which she never really was. Though if you dared to ask her to please keep her eyes on the road, well then she would turn and look at you while she insisted that she had never for even a minute taken her eyes off the road. So he just sat there, prayed to a god he didn't really believe in, and hoped to get where they were going alive.

His day started with Aggy explaining he could have either cold pizza for breakfast or he could have cold pizza. *How does she eat that junk?* He thought. *Without my steel cut oatmeal and live-culture yogurt I won't be able to poop for a week!* He didn't dare say anything about it, though, because he knew she'd tease him unmercifully. So he just ate the cold pizza. He still had sauce and pepperoni caught in his teeth.

Now he regretted his choice of breakfast, wishing instead that he'd opted for a big bowl of nothing at all. Aggy's driving had the pizza doing the Macarena in his otherwise empty gut, and he was afraid he'd hurl at every screeching curve. Unable to help himself he finally yelled, "Jesus Christ, Aggy, slow the fuck down! There isn't a fire."

"Loosen up, Granny!" she barked back. "The kids drive faster than I do. All the campus rent a cop might do is give me a ticket. What's one more?" She pointed at the glove compartment in front of David.

David popped the release and wished he hadn't. Tickets for parking, speeding and who knows what else streamed out of the glove compartment. "Shit, Aggy. It's like I broke the piñata at a kid's birthday party, you know if the kid was a felon." Aggy chuckled and shrugged. David scrambled to shove the tickets back in and slammed the door closed. He scowled at Aggy then settled down in his seat, gripping the "oh shit!" handle above his car door.

Aggy continued driving like a maniac till she screeched to a halt in her assigned parking space at the university lab building. David hopped out before she'd even undone her seat belt and fighting his every instinct walked towards the building instead of dropping to the ground on all fours and kissing the earth.

They cut it, they diced it, they blended it, they put it into a centrifuge. They ran every test known to man on it, yet Aggy still could not find one single reason for it to glow.

David hung over her shoulder like some demented vulture waiting for someone to croak. Then for the third time in twenty minutes he said, "I don't get it. I just don't get it."

"And I do? It's lit up like a firefly's ass but there's no logical reason why." Aggy rolled her eyes. "Whatever would we do without your keen sense of observation?"

"Excuse me for living," David shot back. So she was guessing she had sounded even bitchier than she had meant to.

"Well of course after all that's your parents fault," Aggy said working up a smile.

"We're both tired of banging our heads against the wall getting nowhere," David said. "Maybe we need to take a break for a minute."

"Yes, that's a new idea, 'let's take a break'." Aggy immediately wished she hadn't said it.

"What?" David asked, proving she hadn't said it as loud as she thought she did.

"Nothing." Aggy took a deep breath and let it out. She stood up from her perch on her chair and when she turned nearly ran into him. She backed up quickly. "You're right. We're both tired."

She jumped back so fast he wondered if he had bad breath. *Probably that damn pizza which is still just in there alone not digesting.* Working together was awkward, and they were accomplishing NOTHING. *We are spinning our wheels making a huge, frustrating rut. We have checked and rechecked everything and we can't even figure out how it glows.* "If we can't even figure out how it glows how can we hope to find out how it's affecting those kids?"

"What we know is that the glowing is how it's affecting the kids," Aggy smiled at him as she moved away. "Think like a scientist, David. It's not much but since the elements test safe every time but it glows for no good reason, whatever makes it glow —that's what's screwing up the kids."

I haven't thought like a real scientist since I left school. I'm just a corporate drone a figure head. Why am I really here now? I lost my super cushy job. What can I gain? David considered. *The shit is screwing up kids but big deal I don't even have any kids, so why do I care? Those fucking assholes know there is something wrong with this stuff but it's worse than that; I think they did it on purpose. Maybe I'm losing my mind, but I think there is a huge conspiracy. I can't let these jack asses get away with... well whatever the hell they're doing.*

David grabbed his jacket off the back of a chair and rummaged through his pocket, hoped for a mint and found the end of a well-wrinkled and torn wrapper with one slightly lint-fuzzy mint from a roll he'd bought in a hotel gift shop. *Who the hell pays two bucks for a roll of mints? More to the point who eats something that's been in their pocket so long it has started to morph into something half jacket and half mint?* David popped it into his mouth. *The guy who had cold and stinky pizza for breakfast, that's who.*

"Did you hear me?" Aggy asked in slow concise words.

"No I didn't," he said in exactly the same way. This made Aggy smile.

"I said, maybe we should stop testing and take another look at the information on that drive you hijacked. Our tests aren't working—at least not right now—maybe we missed something in the data."

CHAPTER FOUR

Well That Was a Surprise!

Three days later they had gone over the files umpteen times and run every test they could think of to run and were not one bit closer to finding an answer. The interns had left hours ago as perplexed and, let's face it, bored as she and David were. There was nothing quite like running the same tests over and over again only to get the exact same results.

"This is the very definition of insanity," David said, tugging at his hair which in Aggy's opinion left it looking not much different than the creepy-assed clown that sold this shit.

"Well, Einstein's anyway," Aggy mumbled.

"It's nothing. Milk, vinegar, baking soda, liquid starch, food color, a tiny amount of borax, even if we give the ingredients huge scientific names there is nothing scary in it. Except whatever the fuck makes it glow which... oh by the way doesn't leave a chemical signature. At what point do we just admit we don't fucking know and... I don't know maybe call NASA?"

"You're not helping, David," Aggy said with a grin. "Why don't you go lay down in my office? I just want to wait for the results of this test."

"Yes... I'm sure it will be very fruitful. At least as much as the fifty bazillion other times we ran it."

Aggy grinned. "Still not helping."

He mumbled something and slunk off to her office.

Just for shits and giggles Aggy opened another container of the crap, poured it on to the counter, and just started poking it with a pen. "Glow little glow blob glimmer, glimmer. You're driving me mad so you're the winner! Others tried but they all failed..."

From the office David called, "Aggy are you singing to the Weirdough?"

"Well I was," she muttered.

"What?"

"Yes, David, I was singing it a lullaby! Perhaps it will go to sleep and I can tease the secrets out of it while it's in a vegetative state."

David laughed but didn't say anything else. It seemed to Aggy that things weren't as tense between them, so maybe the fucking shrinks were all wrong and the best way to fix things was just to ignore everything in your past and pretend nothing had happened.

She poked the stuff again then watched as it took its form. That it should do. Its properties were all about staying together, being molded, retaining its shape, bouncing, picking up news print. Perhaps the biggest mystery of Weirdough was that Silly Putty wasn't suing the living shit out of them. They used only slightly different ingredients and the only real difference in the two products was that Weirdough came in a bigger container, there was more of it, and it glowed—which so far she had found not one reason for it to do either that or turn kids into drones.

She didn't remember going to sleep at all. But she woke with a start as memories that weren't hers started to flood her brain. When she looked down the Weirdough was covering her hand and the glow was traveling up her arm. She screamed, focused on forcing the presence from her brain then watched as the Weirdough fell away from her arm, hardened, then turned to dust as fast as she could think it.

David ran in, but the panicked look on his face disappeared as soon as he saw she appeared to be alright. He must have realized just as quickly that she was anything but alright because he moved closer to her.

"What happened?"

"Fuck! Forty billion tests we ran on the shit. Two qualified scientists and two interns spent most of three days running tests using millions of dollars' worth of equipment, and what didn't we do? Leave it out of its fucking box!"

"What happened when you left it out of the box?"

"Shit dried up and turned to dust, but not before it proved the existence of something that... well it just can't be."

David brought Aggy a cup of water and a cool, wet cloth which she immediately wiped her face down with.

Wow she's lost all her color. Aggy has always been pretty unflappable. Even after her attack she didn't react with panic or fear. If she had I don't want to think about what would have happened to her, so I just don't. Afterwards she wasn't jumping at her own shadow; she was just pissed off... at the whole world. What the hell could have happened with the Weirdough to leave Aggy shaking and green?

She threw the cloth down on the table top then downed the water in the cone-shaped paper cup in one gulp. And how had Aggy always dealt with things she didn't want to talk about? She changed the subject usually to something completely absurd.

"I hate these fucking cups. Can't drink part of them and set them down. You can't use them twice. What a lot of waste..."

"Focus, Aggy."

"I *really* wish this was rum. Tequila. Hell, even turpentine. What I need is a good, stiff drink...."

"What the hell happened!"

"It just can't be, it can't," Aggy mumbled and stood. "I'm done in, you're done in, let's call it a day." Then she was immediately shutting the lab down for the night.

David followed her around.

"We get our first real break... Well what might be our first real break and you don't want to talk about it. What the hell happened, Aggy? You know it shouldn't have turned to dust that quickly. It should have taken months. Just tell me what you think you know."

"Yes, guessing is oh so very scientific. Wow you have been up in the industrial chemical towers too long. Down here in real science land we make damn sure we have done enough testing..."

"Dammit, Aggy!" As she walked around him she purposely stepped on his toe, at least he was pretty sure it was on purpose. "What the hell!"

"Sorry." She clearly wasn't at all. "See, I'm so tired I don't even know where I'm stepping. Time to call it a day."

The car ride back to her house was mostly silent. He had tried to get her to tell him just what had happened and what she thought it meant and she had told him not so politely to shut the hell up and leave her alone.

The minute Aggy walked in her door she went straight to the kitchen, got a bottle of rum down and grabbed a couple of glasses. She tossed one at David and he barely caught it, poured herself a bourbon—full to the brim—and yelled more than said as she held the bottle out to him, "Help yourself."

He took the bottle and poured himself a shot.

"Bring that with you," She ordered.

By the time he got to the living room she was flopping on the couch and she had already drunk enough that she didn't spill her drink. She stared into her glass as if booze had an answer different than it had the last time.

David decided to try to disrupt her attempt to drown the finding she found uncomfortable with booze. "Maybe we should eat something? I could order in, what do you want? Please don't say pizza."

Aggy grinned. "Okay, no pizza. There is a good Asian place on the speed dial or there may be some ancient Paleolithic cans of soup in the cabinet. You may need a shovel and pick to find the microwave. It would take a bulldozer to find the cook top, and… It's just easy to eat pizza. No plates to wash no heating necessary, but if you just have to muck things up…"

David shook his head. "I'll order Asian food thank you and don't worry I won't make you wash the containers."

Aggy downed the rest of the glass of rum made a face and poured another from the bottle David had tried to put out of her comfortable reach. She clicked her tongue disapprovingly. "Fine, you just go ahead and build your own hole in the ozone layer then."

"I'll tell them to use paper."

"So many dead trees."

"Hey pizza comes in boxes made from what were once majestic trees."

"You don't know that. They may have been made from ugly, scrawny-assed trees." She grinned.

"Are we really tree shaming now?" David laughed. As he looked for the restaurant number on the phone he looked over at Aggy. Her eyes were already glassy meaning she was mostly already drunk and… *It's the first time she has sounded like the Aggy I knew and loved since I got here. Maybe now's the time to ask her what she learned.*

"Aggy what happened with the Weirdough back at the lab?"

Aggy growled in his direction and ordered, "Jedi mind tricks only work on the weak minded. Just order some stinking food."

"What do you want?"

"You know what I like."

"But I'm not ordering pizza." He laughed.

"You still know what I like, jackass."

"I hope your body doesn't go into shock from vegetable matter entering it."

"Tomatoes are a vegetable."

"Technically they're a fruit."

"So you do remember some things."

Three days later he was no closer to getting her to let go of the goods. Whatever she had found out she wasn't comfortable with, so she just wasn't about to tell him.

Now she was pulling out yet more containers of the crap, opening them and dumping them into fish tanks with wire lids. Periodically she would touch them. For reasons known only to Aggy she kept making him and the interns touch them. Within an hour and a half one by one the Weirdough turned to dust. Which shouldn't have happened any more than it glowed. "Maybe we need to go to sleep, shut ourselves down," she mumbled.

It was so late the interns had already left, each looking at Aggy like she was going mad. David couldn't blame them.

"For the love of that thing people call God, what the hell do you think? I don't care how crazy you think it sounds. It no longer matters; I think you're crazy now anyway."

Aggy took a deep breath, looked him straight in the eyes and said, "You may have to revisit the whole God thing."

"What's that supposed to mean?!"

She seemed to be trying to think of some sane way to say it, and then just blurted it out. "The glowing thing that leaves no chemical or biological signature?"

"Yes?"

"It's an alien soul."

David laughed out loud then looked right at her to see if she was, but she wasn't, not even a grin.

"You're not even saying you think? Aggy we're... we're scientists. There is no such thing as a soul... there is no such thing as aliens."

"I fell to sleep, that shit crawled on me, and before I was fully awake I saw a world not our own. Some kind of... dark planet. It had rings around it and big bands of space dust circling it. It was mostly hollow, gutted by generations of creatures growing and reproducing and using... well everything, just like we do. The planet was dead; we had to leave..."

"We?"

"Don't interrupt me. No one likes to be interrupted especially when they are saying something that sounds bum-fuck crazy even to them. They had used everything, nothing could survive, the very atmosphere was poisoned. There was a machine. It took their souls from their bodies and sealed them into air-tight jars. I saw a lot of bright flashes, like something moving really fast, too fast to see. It made me a little queasy, like a roller coaster with too many loops at top speed, and then I was awake. Awake and aware, I could evict that soul from my body.

"Don't you see? The soul has to be kept in an air-tight container. The Weirdough allows the soul to leave that container, but once the Weirdough starts to dry out—even a little—the soul gets evicted, and with nowhere to go... well I have no idea what happens to it."

"That's just fucking crazy, Aggy!"

"Which is why I didn't want to tell you. I know it sounds crazy. Don't you think I know it sounds crazy?! So I just keep running tests, but I know what I saw and what I felt. When you give me a scientific explanation for why it glows, why children's personalities change, and why it turns to dust, then you can make fun of me. Until then maybe you should try using a crow bar to open your mind just a crack. I suggest you go to sleep and then we take one that's been out for hours..."

"You want to use me as a guinea pig?"

"Well if you think I'm full of shit and my hypothesis is just crazy it shouldn't bother you at all to do it, now should it?"

"I'm still not doing it."

"If you won't do it then you are admitting that you think I may be right and then... Well you have to admit that you are at least as crazy as I am."

David wouldn't agree to the experiment, only—he kept insisting—because it was just silly. He had made it clear as hell that she wasn't going to convince him that she might be right unless he experienced it himself, yet he wouldn't agree to a simple test.

The thing was she didn't really have to have his permission. As a scientist, she knew she needed another test subject. How could he object to that? Well he couldn't for sure if he was asleep.

He was lying on her couch, dead to the world, one hand actually lying on the coffee table. She had kept the crap in her pocket for nearly an hour and a half she pulled it out and sat it near David's right hand. In seconds it enveloped his hand and the light started to go up his arm. She reached over and shook him awake.

Lights, lights rushing in *so fast, can't see! Can't unsee!* David's body felt light, surreal; there was a strange sensation like someone trying to evict him from his own body. At some level he realized the thoughts he was thinking were not his own.

My home, our home, in ruins! The planet swirls with the ashes of our dead, everything in our world laid to waste. Evacuate everyone! Get out while you can! Remember the drill and gather your loved ones! We must leave!

A strange language and yet he understood every word because he was on his way out and something else was taking over his body. David twitched, moaning, hearing the words, knowing their meaning, feeling the dread they carried.

A booming voice shouted instructions and encouragement, *Keep going, follow the plan, we will find a new home we will be saved! We will live again!* He heard wails and screams, some were dying, but others were being transformed in the machine. So many screams, so many screams...

David woke up screaming. He was sweaty and gasping. He blinked his eyes, trying to orient himself to where he was.

Aggy was there, beside him, watching. She was holding an empty Weirdough container and she pointed to its former contents sitting on the coffee table in front of him.

"Quick, David! Before it changes!"

David tried to focus on the blob, it pulsed twice then the light vanished and then poof it turned to dust. Still raw from his experience it took a second for creeping realization to jump up and smack him in the face.

"What the fuck, Aggy? I specifically told you not to do that! Do I have a big sign on my head that says lab rat?"

"Look... Did you really want me to be that crazy all by myself?"

"Yes, yes I did. It... it can't be can it? It just can't be."

"Yeah, that's what I kept saying, and then we ran a bunch more tests. Can you come up with a better explanation for what just happened to you? I'd take anything, anything at all."

"We... we need to run more tests, many, many more tests!"

"To prove what? Towards what end? Did you see it? The dead planet?"

"I saw lights, like you said and space, a planet...." He told Aggy everything he had seen and heard during his experience and then they compared notes.

"I didn't get a good picture of what they looked like, but I definitely got that we weren't dealing with a little cute glowy finger-healing E.T. here." Aggy added, "I'm not sure, but I think there is a chance that they are...."

"Like parasites," David finished. "They have found a way to move their souls... I can hardly say that word without my throat wanting to close up...."

"I know, right?"

"They built a soul-extracting machine..."

"It vacuum-packs them, and now they can move from one host to another." Aggy sighed then looked at him. "So, I'm sorry I stuck the soul-sucking alien on your arm, but if you were me you would have done it, too."

"I would not."

She looked at him, one eyebrow raised and said, "Really? Because I seem to remember I said I could eat the hot pepper sauce without acting like a pussy and then you stuck it on my pizza without me knowing...."

"And you ate it and whined like a little bitch with a skinned knee." He laughed then got mad all over again. "On what planet is sneaking hot sauce on a pizza the same as letting a soul-sucking alien loose on someone!"

"On the planet where there is an alien soul in a kid's toy and I can't be the only one who knows that. I said I was sorry! What do you want, blood?"

"What I want is to go back to a few minutes ago when I just thought you were crazy and had never even for a moment—at least not in my adult life—considered the possibility that there was a soul, much less aliens."

"And now you know how I felt and why I wouldn't tell you."

CHAPTER FIVE

Shut Up and Put That Down

Aggy had sent the interns away two days ago. Now it was just she and David. Shit was getting real up in here, and she was suddenly consumed with paranoia. It was one thing to be dealing with exposing possible contaminants in a product and having a corporate goon squad come after you because you might dip into their very deep pockets and quite another to be screwing with soul-sucking aliens bent on taking over children and maybe through them the world.

"I'm wondering about our ethics, Aggy," David said.

"What?" she said, looking up from where she had been peering through the microscope. She'd had her eye to it so much the last week she was sure it was going to attach itself at any moment. She rubbed her eyes. "What?" she asked again, this time looking at David. His eyes were bloodshot and she was pretty sure sleep-wise he wasn't in any better shape than she was.

"Well..." He pointed to the newest pile of dust on the counter. "That's like the third one of those things we've killed today..."

"Four but who's counting? If there is a soul in each of these—and it's looking like there is—I'm not sure you can actually kill the soul. It just... I don't know... goes somewhere else. Maybe I should have paid attention in Sunday school, but really even as a kid I thought that was a huge waste of time. I should ask Scooter; he's pretty spiritual."

"Scooter, our Scooter? He's still alive?"

"Amazingly so." She grinned. "Actually Scooter is still my best friend. He cleaned up his act—well mostly anyway—years ago. He's very much in tune to a bunch of crap that neither of us understands. He's very rich and kind of crispy on the edges, but I think... well maybe you need to lose most of the left side of your brain to actually think deep and esoteric things."

"Yet you don't think what you are doing is killing these

things?"

"So what if I am? They are taking over the bodies of kids..."

"Why kids?"

"I've been thinking about that. They didn't grab either of us till we were asleep. I think they can't take over an adult because their personality is too strong. The soul is already too connected to the personality. A kid is in a constant state of becoming. They are aware of themselves on a totally different level than we are."

"This is all fucking crazy, Aggy." David sighed. "This shit has only been on the market less than six months and it's already everywhere."

"Well here's something super scary; why aren't all those kids taken over already?"

"What?"

"They could take them over whenever they wanted. Why have they only taken over a couple of dozen kids...?"

"You're right; that is scary."

They had admitted they both needed sleep and that they weren't really learning anything in the lab and had gone back to Aggy's.

David looked at the slice in his hand. He remembered a time when he had liked pizza—he had regular bowel movements, too.

"You know, Aggy, you could order a salad with the pizza."

"Such a mess! Are you going to clean my house?"

"Like you clean your house. I would be surprised if we didn't lift a stack of empty pizza boxes one day and find the skeleton of your cleaning woman under it."

"I've never had a cleaning woman." She looked thoughtful and mumbled, "We might find that cat."

"I knew I smelled a cat."

"Alive or dead?"

"It's hard to tell. Potato, tomato."

"You know what we need?" Aggy asked, starting on a second slice of pizza. The next words out of her mouth were inaudible.

"Seriously, Aggy, maybe if you swallowed the half a slice of pizza you have in your mouth I could hear you."

She swallowed part of it, chipmunked part of it in one cheek and said, "I said what we need is to run tests on some of those kids."

"Are you nuts, Aggy? How would we go about doing that? Knock on their door and tell their parents we believe a kid's toy took over their child?"

"Well that's just insane; a toy can't take you over." Aggy laughed. "I didn't say I knew how to do it just that is what we need to do. Here's an idea; how about you come up with an idea?"

At the lab they had given up on pretending that more tests were going to help them at all and were instead once again going over all the data they had about the kids who had been affected and how they were acting.

Aggy rubbed her eyes and looked over where he was sitting reading a hard copy they had made of the file. Funny a few days ago he had been afraid to even leave the thing open on the computer, and now he had a hard copy that he misplaced half the time.

"So once the presence...."

Aggy interrupted him. "Oh, I like that so much better than soul."

"Me too... Once the presence leaves, the Weirdough turns to dust—which it shouldn't according to its chemical signature. If you dried this stuff and it had never had a resident alien, it would just be a dried, cracked, chunk of putty. It would eventually turn to dust but it would probably take years."

"When the presence leaves there is nothing but dust. How the hell does it do that?"

"No clue," David said. Why was he no longer worried that he was going to be arrested for corporate espionage? Those aliens weren't going to call the police; the last thing they wanted to do was draw attention to themselves or their "product." If they thought he was a real problem they wouldn't have fired him they would have killed him. If they knew he had the files or that he had a clue as to what they were doing they would have already come after him. They hadn't which meant they weren't worried about him.

"You know these aliens are pretty cocky. Obviously they aren't worried about being caught at all."

"And another one bites the dust," Aggy said, with a weird cross between laughter and jubilation.

David looked over at the fish tank with the screen top that

normally would have held a rat and winced.

"I still don't feel good about that." Aggy had been sticking one of the blobs of Weirdough after another into the tank all day and timing how long it took them to die. It was always nearly an hour and a half, so she was mostly just getting some form of sadistic pleasure from it.

"It's all in the name of science. I'm sorry, but I don't really think American homes need to be filled with the pitter-patter of little aliens," Aggy said as she dumped another blob into the tank and put the lid on it. All the stuff could do was roll one way or the other, so the top was over kill. "What we really need is to start talking to those kids."

"How? What excuse would we use?"

"You know, David, I can't do all the thinking around here. I'm doing all the work—you know dumping the crap out, watching it turn to dust, doing a little dance of joy because I have killed one more."

"Dammit, Aggy, I really don't think we should be killing them. We don't really know what they want here…"

"And that is the crap right there, David. We both know. We saw it; we know exactly what they want to do. They don't care about killing any of us to live, and they are no more deserving than we are. I had forgotten how selectively stupid you can be."

"What the hell is that supposed to mean?"

"What part of an alien invasion fleet is taking over children do you just not understand? You constantly want to worry about everyone's fucking rights, but you forget that some people only think they have rights if they are allowed to persecute other people."

"So we're back to that. I wouldn't go kill the bastard that attacked you or let you do it, so I'm some sort of bleeding-heart dove."

There was only a second when David was glad he had said it because he felt like the whole thing was just hanging between them. He immediately wished he hadn't said it, and he was pretty sure Aggy was about to hand him his ass in a hat box. But before she could fire her word torpedo the door to the lab opened, and because of the fight they were having—that was about to get really nasty—they both jumped.

The man walked in like he owned the place. He was tall and fairly thin but had a pot belly that made him look like he was pregnant; he was bald as a billiard ball but had a full red beard that reached to the middle of his chest. He was wearing a tattered green T shirt with a bright yellow pot leaf emblazoned on it, cargo shorts and leather sandals. When he smiled and it went all the way to his blue eyes David knew who it was before Aggy said. "Scooter!" and ran over to hug him.

"You old son of a bitch I haven't seen you in weeks how the hell are you?"

"Alright, mostly. You know how this time of year is right before the holidays. Ex-wives all arguing about where I'm supposed to be and what I'm supposed to do with who when. All with their hands out because it's the holidays and there are gifts to buy for... well I lost count of how many kids and grandkids. Half the time I don't know which ones I'm actually related to, but there are a lot of the little bastards, and I know they ain't all mine, but damn I hate to hurt anyone's feelins' specially around the holidays."

He released Aggy and looked at David, David smiled and Scooter laughed. "Hot damn, Dave!" He walked over and gave David a big bear hug.

David gave him a one-arm hug, patted him twice on the back implying that he was done with the hug, but no Scooter just kept holding him till it was awkward and a little unsettling.

When Scooter finally let him go and stepped back his head started to pop around like a bobble head in a car window and he said, "Man, is this a blast from the past or what? You know I always knew you two would find your way back to each other."

"David's just here for work, Scooter," Aggy said, and leaned around Scooter to give David a go-to-hell-go-straight-to-hell-don't-pass-go-don't-collect-your-two-hundred-dollars look that would build an ice burg in the middle of a desert.

"What are you up to?"

"Well Aggy I know you aren't a medical doctor, but as you know I don't trust those quacks. My oldest son Alex... You remember, he's the one that's such an embarrassment?"

"I remember."

"Well his kid Blake." He looked at David and rolled his eyes. "What the fuck kind of name is that Blake? Are we on Dynasty or some shit? Any way Blake started acting weird about a week ago. Now I had just visited a few days before and Alex had the nerve to ask me if I had left anything there, which I didn't. So I went to see what he was talking about and... Well that little bastard is usually bouncin' off the walls screamin' like a banshee and runnin' up and down the halls, throwing shit around the house like a rabid-ass yard ape... You know just a lot of fun. No kiddin' this kid could tear up a steel ball with a butter knife. I get there and the little fucker opens the door and says, 'Good evening, Grandfather, how are you?"

"What's wrong with that?" David asked.

"What's wrong? Till right then I didn't even know the little fucker could talk at least not with words. Normally I walk in and he's like a ten-armed octopus climbing all over me going through all my pockets looking for gum and money. It's been a week now and he's still all... well polite and stuff. 'Would you care for some tea, Grandfather? Would you like a muffin, Grandfather?' I'm tellin' you he's creeping me right the fuck out. 'Children of the candy corn' and all that crap."

"Did he have some Weirdough?" David asked.

"I told them and now I'm telling you, I didn't have any drugs in their house and I sure as hell didn't let that demented little monkey have any." He looked at Aggy and grinned. "You know my motto, Aggy. Never waste good drugs on kids."

"It is a good motto. He's talking about Weirdough the toy. He means this." Aggy held up an empty container.

"Hell I don't know. If every other kid has it he probably does. They are all about giving him whatever he wants just to get him to shut his pie-hole." He looked at Aggy. "You know how those kind of people are. 'Here's a ribbon, here's a cookie. Did you get your little feelings hurt today? Let me buy you a bunch of crap so that you'll feel better'." Scooter sighed. "I'm worried about him, Aggy. He just isn't acting like himself. Do you have any ideas?"

"This crap..." Aggy shook the container in the air. "Contains an alien presence that has been taking over kids."

"You're shittin' me."

"Nope, watch." She pointed to the tank. The trapped blob started rolling back and forth, looking for a host.

"Is it supposed to do that?" Scooter asked.

"Nope."

It pulsed a couple of times and then turned to dust.

Scooter rubbed at his chin through his beard leaving the hairs standing in every direction. "And that's a kid's toy?"

"Yep. With an alien presence in it," Aggy answered.

"You mean like a soul?" Scooter asked.

Aggy sighed, rolled her eyes and said grudgingly, "Yes like a soul." she grinned then. "But don't call it that; it makes David very uncomfortable."

Scooter turned to David, and even before he started talking David knew Aggy had just thrown him under the bus.

"You know, David, science explains so little when we talk about who and what we really are. Why do we zig instead of zag, go left instead of right? Earth is just like a school for our cosmic soul, man. Why do we live? Why do we die? How many licks does it take to get to the chocolate center of a lollipop? There is so much that science just cannot explain..."

As Scooter continued to dribble stupid all over the lab, David caught Aggy's eye and mouthed the words, *I'm sorry please make it stop now.*

"Hey, Scooter, I hate to interrupt, but maybe we'd better have a look at your grandson the sooner the better."

CHAPTER SIX

Well, Snap!

David leaned up and whispered in Aggy's ear, "Tell me why we are in Scooter's pot van and he's driving?"

Aggy turned her head and said, "Because I don't know where we're going, do you? Plus the alien has seen Scooter and this van before, so he's not going to speak and tell the hive mind."

"Hive mind?" David said.

"They might have a hive mind." Aggy shrugged. "We don't really know. Do you want to risk it?"

David sat back in his seat and re-adjusted his seat belt. "I don't know that would be any bigger risk than riding with a stoner," David mumbled.

As for not drawing attention to themselves, turned out Aggy wasn't just talking out her ass. Scooter really was rich and how did he get that way? When pot became legal in Colorado he started growing it legitimately instead of in his closet with grow lights and his own urine. Scooter now had hundreds of acres of pot farms and supplied not only the five store fronts he had in Colorado but thousands of dispensaries all over the country wherever medicinal marijuana was legal.

They were now driving around in a huge, neon-yellow panel van with a huge pot leaf painted on the side back panel and a cartoon version of Scooter giving a big thumbs-up. In neon green letters it said, "Smoke 'em if ya got 'em. And if you don't got 'em, I doobie, doobie do!" He might as well have a bigger sign that said *I'm a dope head! Please pull me over!*

When they pulled into the drive way, David saw a nice ranch-style, well-landscaped, two-car garage, upper middle class house.

"Ah, Scooter, why is Alex such a disappointment?"

"Look at this place, man! He's a sell-out; he works for the man. He's a fucking accountant for some corporation. A corporation! He plays racket ball, he eats brie. His dog is on Xanax, he drinks pumpkin spice lattes. He's one of *those* people, drone to society. He keeps his soul in a box, just like those aliens. I didn't raise him to be like this, man. Of course I didn't really raise him, his mama did so... not my fault."

The man who opened the door was dressed and moved just as Scooter had described him.

You know, just like David. Aggy grinned and thought about telling Scooter what David had been doing for the last twenty years. Alex looked just like Scooter when he had hair on his head but not on his face. There was no mistaking whose kid this was, so Aggy knew exactly why he was such a disappointment. He looked just like Scooter so he couldn't disown him and he was everything Scooter hated.

"What do you want, Dad?" Alex asked. Obviously the feelings of disappointment were shared by father and son alike.

"Peace of mind." Scooter laughed at his joke then frowned. "How's about a little respect for your old man?"

Alex stared at him with a look Aggy normally saved for vacuum cleaner salesmen or Jehovah's witnesses. "What do you want, Dad?"

"Whatever happened to a dad just dropping by for a visit, huh? I wanted you to meet some old college friends of mine, David and Aggy."

Alex stood aside and gestured for them to enter. As they walked through his door he sighed as if they had just asked to move in with a rat and three St. Bernard dogs. When they stepped into the sunken living room area they were joined by a slim, stylishly dressed young woman that Alex introduced as his wife, Kirstie.

"That's KIR-stie, not KRI-stie," she said, with a friendly smile. She was the female version of her husband.

When the couple were seating themselves on the far side of the room, Scooter turned to David and Aggy threw up his hands and said, "See what I mean?"

David and Aggy took a place on the loveseat as Scooter plopped down on an overstuffed armchair. When Scooter slung his leg over the arm of the chair the cargo shorts he was wearing didn't leave much to the imagination in that he obviously wasn't wearing underwear. Aggy grinned and thought, *well at least I know why he always had some good-looking woman running along after him.*

"Dad for the love of God, your junk is hanging out."

Scooter didn't move his leg much less blush. He just reached down and stuffed his stuff back into his pants as if he just couldn't understand why his son was being so stuffy.

Aggy looked down and grinned. She loved Scooter, but it couldn't be easy to be one of his kids especially not if you wanted to live the way Alex did.

"David and Aggy are doctors…"

"Dad, I told you I'm not giving Blake pot."

"They ain't that kind of doctors."

He turned to David and Aggy. "Why do kids always have to look down on what their parents do for a living? It's not like I'm running hookers on the corner and don't think I couldn't I got a pimp hat, and a back-hand slap that could pop a bitch's eye right out."

He turned back to his son. "I told them about your little dumplin' Blake and how he seems a little off. He's obviously still not himself after all I don' hear screamin' and my keys and wallet are still in my pockets."

"Excuse me," Alex said to her and David, then turned back to Scooter.

"Dad, I don't remember asking you to interfere with my son."

"No offense," he said to Aggy and David, "but I don't want my son exposed to any of my dad's hippie shit."

"*Our* son," corrected Kirstie. She looked at Aggy and Aggy could see the fear in her eyes. This was a woman worried sick about her child, worried enough that she was willing to let strangers look at him if that's what it took. "Our son isn't himself, but when we took him to his pediatrician he said there was nothing wrong with him."

"Of course, *our* son." Now she could hear the nerves in Alex's voice, too.

"I'm worried about little dumpling. He's not himself, is he Kristie?" Scooter said.

Kirstie gritted her teeth and said, "KIR-stie, Dad. it's KIR-stie, not KRI-stie."

Scooter waved a hand dismissively. "Yeah, yeah. Look, my friends have some questions for you. You know things like do you think he's acting so weird because maybe one of his toys was filled with an alien soul and it took him over and now he's possessed… You know something like that?"

Beside her she saw David mouth the words *I'm so sorry* to Alex.

"What the hell, Dad?" Alex said. "That's the goofiest thing you've ever said which... makes it monumental. Did you take a great big bong hit before you got here?"

"We really are doctors," Aggy said, "and we do have some questions. For instance did your son by any chance come into contact with the toy Weirdough?"

"He had some... he lost it. Is there something wrong with it?" Kirstie asked.

"It holds an alien soul!" Scooter said. "But yeah, I'm the one who's high. You gave your kid an alien soul to play, with but I'm a bad parent."

"Is it toxic?" Alex asked with real concern. "Dad is right..."

"I bet that hurt ya," Scooter said with a laugh.

Alex ignored his father. "Blake isn't himself at all."

"What exactly is he doing?" David asked.

As the parents started running down a long list—not unlike the ones they already had on file—of the way their child had changed, Aggy sort of checked out. She looked around the room. *This looks just like a perfect magazine-style house. They don't have any weird cat smells here. Look at that big screen television! Don't kids leave things everywhere? So is mommy a little OCD or does the alien just always pick up all his toys and... Who knows? Maybe it's easier to raise an alien than a human kid, maybe everyone will want one.*

David was fidgeting like a squid on hot sand. When Aggy turned to look at him she saw, out of the corner of her eye, a small, freckled-faced little boy peering around the corner out of the hall. When she looked at him, full on so that he knew he had been seen, he ducked his head quickly and disappeared.

"Excuse me," Aggy interrupted "May I use your restroom? Late nights, too much coffee, you know how it is."

"Oh I know," Kirstie said. "I love my pumpkin spice lattes, but they go right through me. Go down the hall, second door on the left."

Aggy got up and went in the direction Kirstie pointed—which was just where she wanted to go in the first place. In the hall way the door at the end on the left slammed quickly shut, and she walked right past the bathroom and up to the boy's door.

She paused for only a moment, just long enough to pull her gun out of the holster in the top of her pants, then slung the door open. The child-looking thing jumped and then cringed. He started to scream, but she showed it the gun.

"You'd better keep your mouth shut you little weirdo!" She thought about the irony of that for a minute but let it go. "What happens to the kid when you take over their body?"

It just stared at her and she realized what she had done.

"Alright you can open your mouth to talk but don't you dare scream."

"I have no idea what it is you are speaking about madam. Perhaps your blood sugar is low. Would you care for a muffin?"

"Here's a clue for you, alien slime. Children don't speak with perfect diction; they don't worry about people's blood sugar or their bowel movements. They are selfish little shits that eat too much candy and only ever half way wipe their asses. They jump on the beds, break everything their parents care about, and shave the cat… well maybe that was just me. My point is I know next to nothing about kids, but I still know more than you do."

He tried to run past her, and she grabbed him and stuck her gun to his head.

"I'm going to ask you questions and you're going to answer them. When you took over this kid's body where did his presence go?"

"You mean his soul?"

Aggy sighed and then said, "Yes, yes you demented little shit. Where is his soul?"

"In here with me. He is annoying and cries all the time."

"Are you trying to take over our planet?"

"We just want to live. Don't you creatures want to live? Well so do we."

"Alright but if the soul is a real thing wouldn't you like to go to some other place? Why would you choose to live in jars and Weirdough or take over little kids?"

"I have learned in my small time here that many of your people believe the afterlife is either all good or all bad. Our people believe that there is an all-good and all-bad after life, but we don't know whether we will go to the good or bad place so… We choose not to die."

With every word he said he pissed Aggy off a little more. Without even really being aware she was doing it her gun was pressed ever harder into his head.

"You... you are hurting me," he said.

She started to ease up then realized something that the aliens didn't. "So... you take over little kids because it's easy to push their soul and their personality to the back, but what you didn't count on is that a kid is easy for an adult to overpower."

"When you hurt me you hurt the boy."

"Ah, but I only have your word for that. I only have your word that the boy is in there at all. You aren't going to let him have a life, and I have no idea how many of you there are or where you will stop if allowed to stay in your host." Aggy was thoughtful for a moment. "I'm just going to have to kill this body, that's all. Then in our atmosphere for—what is it about a second—and *poof!* You have to go off to... well wherever your souls go... You know I'm thinking taking over the bodies of another specie's children isn't going to make you well loved by any deity if such a thing exists so..."

She cocked the gun.

CHAPTER SEVEN

Put That Down; It's Expensive

David watched as the boy came running into the room ran over and hugged first his mother and then his father then promptly ran over to Scooter and started going through his pockets pulling out his keys and then his wallet.

Aggy walked into the room smiling and winked at David.

David was more confused than ever. Then he remembered they were dealing with crazy Scooter... but his son and daughter-in-law had been just as convinced and there was obviously nothing wrong with this kid now that a mega dose of Ritalin wouldn't fix.

Alex looked relieved. "What happened? He's himself again."

Aggy looked over at the boy, who was going through Scooter's wallet and trying to pocket the bills he had gotten from it, grinning. "Well it's amazing what you learn if you just talk to a kid."

Kirstie asked, "What did he say?"

"Well, seems that Blake here thought it would be a good idea to eat his Weirdough. I had the antidote David and I developed in the lab with me and figured it couldn't do any harm to give it to him. He said it tasted gross but he seemed to come right back to being a normal kid after that, though why that's an improvement I'll never know."

"Blake, what did Daddy tell you about your toys?" Alex asked his son, who was busy building a bird's nest in Scooter's beard with money.

The boy looked thoughtful for a moment then said, "Don't touch that, it's expensive."

"The other thing," Alex prompted.

The four-year-old seemed to think for a moment then said, "Don't eat things I can't poop out," Blake mimicked his father's tone.

"That's right, Blake. If it's not food don't eat it," said Alex. He looked at Aggy, "I can't thank you enough. We were so worried. The doctor said he was fine but it was like having a different kid in the house. You think the thing you want most for your kids is to behave but... not when they are so different."

When David looked at Kirstie tears were running down her face.

"There was a bad thing in my head," Blake said.

"Are they going to pull this stuff off the market? Do we need to file a law suit?" Alex asked.

"Yuppie bullshit," Scooter scoffed then mumbled, "aliens are taking over kids! Yeah, a team of lawyers is going to save us. Stupid ass."

"Ah... that's what we're working on now," David said quickly. "Getting all the information together to support a lawsuit."

"We are?" Scooter said. "What about the aliens?"

David looked at Alex and rolled his eyes. "We will want to talk to you again at some point, to make sure Blake is alright and to put you in the file for the suit we are building against Weirdough, Inc."

"We have to get back to the lab and make more of the antidote," Aggy said, herding him and Scooter towards the door. "Your child isn't the only one that has been affected. He should be fine now but call us if you notice any change in behavior..."

"Shouldn't they recall this stuff as soon as possible?" Alex asked.

"I wish it was that simple. We are talking billions of dollars. They'll just say he used the product improperly; it says don't eat it. This is a big company and the product isn't actually toxic," Aggy said. "We have to prove there is a hazard. You need to keep this to yourself for now. I'm sure you understand all about the burden of proof. At this point it's our word against theirs. Do this the wrong way and you'll be the ones facing a lawsuit."

"We understand," Alex said.

"We have friends and family whose kids have this stuff," Kirsti said sniffling. "We can't just let them keep the stuff."

"I suggest you go to their house, find the toy, and flush it down the nearest commode. You don't need to tell them you got rid of it. Maybe start a conversation about hearing the toy had been linked to autism so they don't buy more."

"They'll believe that because everything is these days," Scooter said.

Kirstie nodded.

"We really must go," Aggy said.

Scooter disentangled himself from the boy, kissed his cheek and sat him down. He started pulling the money out of his beard and stuffing it in his pocket.

Alex and Kirstie walked them to the door.

"Seriously thank you so much," Kirstie said. "I make a mean pumpkin spice latte if you're ever in our neighborhood."

"I hope you can stop those bastards," Alex said, "If you need anything from us all you have to do is ask. We'll go to court, write up my statement, whatever it takes."

Scooter hugged his son's neck and kissed his cheek. Then he stepped back and grinning said, "See Alex what did I tell you? You may think your old man is a burned out lay about, but I have mad connections."

As soon as Scooter backed the van out of the drive way David said, "So was the kid alien possessed, Aggy?"

"Yes," Aggy said.

"What the hell did you do? Did you have an exorcist in your fucking pocket!?"

"I talked to it. It told me the kid was in there with it, but there was no way of proving that so... I gave it a choice. It could die with its host or climb into the basic Weirdough I had made in the lab when I was trying to figure out what made the crap glow."

"You threatened a child?!"

"No I threatened a thug-assed alien that took over a kid's body. What would you have done? Made it tea and cookies and asked it politely to tell you the details of the alien's invasion?"

"What exactly did you do, Aggy? I'm pretty sure it didn't just get in the goo because you threatened to read it your thesis on clean crap."

"That's right, make fun of my life's work, and what did you do with your life... oh, I know! You helped aliens take over kids."

"Not on purpose! What did you do Aggy?"

"I smashed a gun to his head and ordered him to get the fuck out."

"Christ Aggy you threatened to kill Scooter's grandson."

"I'm alright with that," Scooter said.

David ignored him. "Aggy... would you have shot him?"

"I don't know. It didn't try me. I might have, and I think we have already established you have no right to judge anyone."

"Dude she's got you there." Scooter laughed. "You got to look at the big esoteric picture, David. Blake was trapped in his own body with an invader, that's harsh for anyone much less a four-year-old. I'm all about finding a peaceful solution. Love is real power. Sometimes it takes a big ugly to make things right. I don't want to hurt a soul but even I know some times you have to kick a little ass and take a few names."

Back in the lab they all looked at the Weirdough container that now held the alien... *presence*... that had possessed the little dumplin' currently known as Blake.

"What should we do with it?" Aggy asked.

"I figured you'd throw it into the tank like all the others just to watch it die," David said, giving her a disapproving look as if she daily went out and ate babies.

"That's alright with me," Scooter said from where he was looking over her shoulder.

"This one we got out of a human body, and I've already talked to it enough to know that it loves nothing more than it does itself. If we could put it into something else...."

"You have about a bajillion rats. Why not put it into one of those?" Scooter suggested.

"That's actually a really good idea," David said, looking shocked.

Aggy took a deep breath and let it out. *David is still incapable of seeing beyond his initial opinion of someone. Scooter didn't get filthy rich because he's an unimaginative idiot.*

"Rats can't talk." Aggy was thoughtful. She was pretty sure that if the alien took over something that didn't have the ability to speak it wouldn't be able to either and there were lots of questions she wanted to ask it. Things like why they could speak English. It couldn't just be because it made it easier to write the script like in every science fiction show she'd ever seen. There had to be some reason why something that had been living suspended in a container for possibly eons knew their language. Suddenly she had a brilliant idea. "Let's go buy a parrot!"

I've been magically *transported back in time!* Aggy thought as she listened to Scooter and David rattling a mile a minute as they made their way to the nearest pet store. *They haven't changed at all; they're still dorks!* She had let David ride shotgun so he'd stop whining about being car sick. *Funny how selective his "motion sickness," is. If he wants to ride in the back he doesn't have it at all. His science is all wonky.*

The two seemingly adult men were deeply engaged in a battle of who could remember the most lines from the Monty Python "dead parrot" skit nearly as old as they were. *Yes, because the existence of our very species doesn't hang in the balance. If humanity is depending on us to save it... well it's totally screwed.*

Aggy tried to concentrate on exactly what kind of parrot they would need. *All it really needs to do is be able to talk. It doesn't even have to be a bird that already talks. Parrots are expensive and when I get fired for missing one lecture after another over the last few weeks I'm not going to have a lot of cash.* It was hard to come up with a genius plan while Tweedle Dumb and Tweedle Dumber talked over each other with bad British accents.

"He is an ex parrot!" said David.

"He has ceased to be!" yelled Scooter.

"He's just having a bit of a rest."

"He is dead I tell you, dead!"

"He's gone to Valhalla! He's pushing up the daisies."

"He's pining for the Fords!"

"Wait a minute. I don't think that's right."

"No? What is it?"

"I think it's fjords."

"Whaddya mean? What's a fjord?"

"It's like a waterway. 'Pining for the Fords?' Why would a dead parrot pine over a car?"

"Why would a dead parrot do anything?"

"You're right." David paused, then, "He's left the building!"

"Shut it, you stooges!" Aggy yelled from the back seat. "I'm trying to make a list of what we need to keep an alien-possessed bird."

"Come on Aggy, jump in. You come up with one," said Scooter.

When he said it Aggy was a little shocked to realize that the reason she was getting so pissed off at them was that she didn't like sharing her friend. After all she was the one who had put up with Scooter for the last twenty years through all his many divorces and other tribulations. David had left them both and now they were acting as if nothing had happened and no time had passed. "How about… he's as dead as two chuckle heads that bugged the shit out of a scientist who had a gun," Aggy said with a laugh.

"That's not very funny," Scooter said, confused.

"Not too harsh your mellow, and I realize it's not as important as reliving that last time you were stoned together, but I'm trying to figure out how to stop the alien invasion of our planet."

David looked at Scooter and nearly giggled. "Yes with a parrot." They both laughed like it was the funniest thing they'd ever heard.

Aggy sighed, *Yep humanity is just screwed.* "Do either one of you dumbasses have a better idea?"

The inaudible mumbling noises they made proved they didn't.

"I'm wondering what sort of cage we're going to need for our alien-possessed parrot. We will need to be able to latch it, and it can't be just any latch because this will not be just any parrot."

"I already feel sort of sorry for the parrot. I mean he has a little birdie life and you're just going to sort of feed him to the alien," Scooter said.

"Yes, poor bird I get it. Focus, big picture, Scooter. A regular clip latch on a cage can be easily flipped even by a regular bird if it works hard enough, and I'm sure once that alien is in a new host it will do anything in its power to get away from us. We're going to need something strong because we sure don't want to risk releasing an alien-possessed parrot on the city or even in the lab."

Scooter made a snorting noise. "Sounds like a bad sci-fi movie—The Parrot That Ate Everything. Wow, man! I just remembered we used something like that to make a commercial for our pot. It wasn't a parrot it was a stoner but scary close." He looked far away then added, "It was like a sign of things to come."

"Good focusing there, Scooter," Aggy mumbled.

"Maybe we should just get a dog crate. They're super strong and roomy… for a bird not a dog. A dog is a wolf you know that? Shouldn't put a wolf in a cage man," Scooter said. "People are in cages too, man. Corporations make cages for people.

They own everything or want to. I had to come up with millions of dollars to start my farm. They do that shit on purpose to keep the little man down."

"Where did you get the money?" David asked

"Oh don't ask that, it will take the rest of the night," Aggy said with a sigh.

"Besides it's better if you don't know—plausible deniability and all."

"Between the bird and the accessories for the bird this is sounding like a pretty expensive venture," David said.

Aggy wondered why David was worried about money. *Probably owes more money than he makes, and now he has no job. That car he drives costs more than I make in a year.* "Who cares? Scooter's paying for everything."

"Me...Why me?" Scooter laughed.

Aggy pointed to herself, "Scientist." Then David, "Unemployed scientist." Then at Scooter, "Multi-million-dollar pot dealer. You do the math."

"No fair! I have to pay just because you two took the wrong path in life?"

"Yes, we took the wrong paths. Don't forget I saved your grandson from life as a grunt for an alien presence," Aggy said.

"Soul," Scooter corrected with a grin.

"No matter what you say you're still paying!" Aggy laughed, finding her sense of humor again. "As anyone with obscene amounts of money should." Because of course that was the speech Scooter had given her any time she tried to pay for anything since he got rich. She took a deep breath and let it out. David acted like she had enjoyed pistol whipping that kid but she hadn't. The truth was it made her sick in her heart and sicker in her stomach. In fact she had nearly hurled the pizza she had for lunch. The memory of the taste in the back of her throat nearly made her decide that David was right about her all-pizza diet. If she could have thought of another way she would have done it. She did what she had to do. Desperate times called for desperate measures, and David should know that after all he had shoved a flash drive up his ass... She may just remind him of that the next time he got all judgmental on her.

"I'll pay, but I get to name it."

"I imagine the alien already has a name. It's not going to

stay a parrot. He's not going to appreciate being called Polly."

"I feel sorry for the bird," Scooter said again.

"Because Aggy will just torture it for information?" David said, thus affording Aggy the opportunity to put her plan into action.

"He might just tell us what we want to know without torturing him, flash drive ass." As she expected, that shut David up. "If he's too much trouble we can just kill him; it's not like it's a kid."

"And *then* it will cease to be!" Scooter said without missing a beat.

"An ex-parrot!"

"You already said that!"

Aggy shook her head. *One is going grey the other is bald as a billiard ball and they both have middle-aged spread yet no doubt they have forgotten important things but this shit they remember.* Aggy gave up on getting anything useful out of either of her cohorts, pulled her smart phone out of her pocket and started making a list of things they'd need to pick up in addition to the parrot. *This has been one long-assed day. I wonder when I'm actually going to get some real sleep and go back to my real job. How long can I send one of my interns to lecture in my place before I get reprimanded? With my tenure it would be damn hard for them to shit-can me. Does any of that matter if aliens take over the planet?*

"This parrot is fine; he's just taking a nap."

"He's dead I tell you."

"He's standing on his perch."

"You nailed his feet to the perch."

"I didn't."

"You did."

God help us all, Aggy sighed and thought yet again, *just screwed.*

"That's nearly everything on our list," Aggy said.

"I have a lovely cage over here very sturdy enamel coated stainless steel with four perches, food and water dishes..."

"We're happy with the dog crate."

"But..." the clerk started, "...it's really not designed for birds. It's... well it's for *dogs*," she said slowly. She obviously thought they might be some of God's special people. While Scooter might be, Aggy and David certainly weren't. *No... we're scientists buying a parrot so we can put an alien soul in it so we can get information from it... No, that doesn't sound crazy at all. We deserve to be talked to like imbeciles.*

They got some bird food and then Scooter started picking up all kinds of stuff as if he were really buying a pet.

"Scooter," Aggy whispered in his ear. "We don't need a bunch of crap for the bird, remember?"

"I feel sorry for the bird, Aggy. It might as well enjoy the last few minutes he has while his little birdy brain is still driving his little birdy body."

David grinned and Aggy shook her head and let Scooter get whatever he wanted. After all it was his money what did she care?

"Is this going to be your bird?" the clerk asked Scooter.

"Um...no. I'm getting it for my grandma. She's so lonely in the home with no one to talk to. See she has bad gas and the other old folks won't even play cards with her," Scooter said. "Didn't they use birds in mines to warn the people when there was bad gas? The bird should be alright, with the gas I mean, right?"

Aggy and David stared at him.

"Aren't you a sweetie? The bird should be fine," said the clerk. "But you'll want to stop by our grooming shop and have his beak and claws trimmed and his wing feathers cut back. We wouldn't want your grandma getting scratched or bitten would we?"

"Yeah, Grandma may smell bad but otherwise she's a delicate flower of femininity." Scooter grinned and winked at her.

Aggy gritted her teeth. *Oh my God! The idiot is flirting with her! We don't have time for this shit. But we do need that bird to be as subdued as possible.* She forced a smile and said, "We'd better get him all trimmed up before we take him to your grandma, Scooter. Can you do that pretty fast? We'd like to get to the home before they shut Grandma in for the evening... She tends to wander."

"Which let me tell you makes the people in the home run for cover." Scooter laughed.

They loaded everything in the van. Aggy found herself sharing the back seat with the parrot.

"Scooter, what the hell was that back there?" David asked.

"Dude, force of habit. When I'm doing something the least

bit sketchy I just start lying. It's like Stoner Tourette's."

The clerk had told them the bird was at least as intelligent as a four or five-year-old and would easily learn to talk. It was a beautiful yellow-headed Amazon. He was sort of singing and chirping, and Aggy found that she was starting to feel sorry for the bird, too until it found the fucking bell Scooter had bought it.

"*Ding, ding! Ding, ding! Ding, ding!*" The bird kept hitting the little bell.

Great. He's toddler smart and the first thing we get is that he knows how to ring the bell.

Scooter slowed the van. "Where is it, man?"

"What?" asked David.

"Ice cream truck, man. Can't you hear that? I keep hearing it but I don't see it. I've been around the block three times already," Scooter said.

"Dammit, burn boy, there is no ice cream truck! There is just this fucking bird ringing the bell you insisted he have."

"Man that is sad—the bell tolls for him."

"Actually Ice cream sounds pretty good right about now," David said, making Aggy wonder if he was getting a contact high just riding in Scooter's van.

Ding, ding! Ding, ding! rang the little bell. *Damn, now that they said it I want ice cream, too.* "Fine, go by the fucking ice cream place, then straight back to the lab."

"How are we going to do this?" David asked Aggy.

"We put the Weirdough in the tank and then put the bird in," Aggy said.

"I can't watch, man. It's so harsh," Scooter said.

"We don't have to, remember? The pet store girl said if we covered his cage he'd go to sleep," David said. He didn't want to see it, either.

"The parrot's soul will be riding shot gun. Maybe we can find a way to get the alien out of the bird later," Aggy said. The ice cream cone she held in her fist dripped onto the notes in front of her making them unreadable and of course she did nothing to clean it up.

David smiled, *She never was all that tidy, but she's become a complete slob.*

They had just covered the tank with a sheet then dumped the Weirdough and parrot inside when Scooter yelled out,

"Wait! He must know his real name before he is taken over, it's the least we can do! He needs to know someone cares that he has a name."

Aggy sighed. "So name him already."

"I can't think of anything."

"What about test subject one?" Aggy suggested.

"Where's your soul, Aggy? Oh I remember you don't believe you have one." Scooter was thinking so hard you could almost see the smoke running out of his ears. Then he shouted out. "Doobie!" he got right up next to the sheet covered tank and said, "Go with grace little Doobie, what you do, you do for all humankind. We'll always remember you ringing your bell wondering why you were riding in someone's car in a dog cage. God's speed little man. May flights of birdie angels wing you to your rest."

"Christ Scooter, he's not a dead parrot," Aggy said.

She looked at David and winked.

David nodded.

"He's just having a nap," David said.

"He's not pushing up the daisies." Aggy's British accent was only slightly better than his.

"He's not pining for the Fords."

"Or even the Chevys."

Scooter turned to look at them and shook his head. "What is wrong with you two? Did someone hurt you when you were little?"

From inside the covered tank a small voice said, "Hello, hello! It's very dark, and I'd like a muffin."

CHAPTER EIGHT

Muffin Top

They had moved the parrot from the tank to the cage and padlocked the door.

Aggy looked in at him. "Does alien want a cracker?"

"My name is Doobie."

"No it isn't! How dare you foul his name... Though he was a bird but that is fowl with a W, I think," Scooter said, looking confused.

"But..." The alien in Doobie's body started. "I like the name Doobie. Be a lamb and fetch me a muffin would you?"

"It's creepy," David said.

"Is that your scientific opinion?" Aggy asked with a grin.

"Pretty sure it is," David said.

"I'm..." The parrot in the cage started to stretch its wings—well what was left of them. "Magnificent. I like this much better than the boy. Can I have a muffin?"

"What's with the muffins?" Aggy asked.

"I like them."

"Do we call him a bird or an alien?" David asked

"You know for all our sakes let's just call him a bird," Aggy said.

David and Scooter nodded.

"I blame Kristie," Scooter said.

"Kirstie," David corrected.

Scooter shrugged. "She's always making these sugar-free bran muffins. They taste like crap. That's how they knew there was something wrong with Blake; he started eating them."

"Bleah," Aggy said.

"What's wrong?" Scooter asked.

"Aliens in the Weirdough and I hate bran muffins."

"I bet you'd like them if they were pizza flavored," David teased.

"Muffin! Right here!" demanded the parrot.

"Enough with the muffin talk, bird. We need some serious

answers. I'm going to ask questions; you're going to answer," Aggy said.

"I'm not talking until I get my muffin."

"Oh, you'll talk or I'll pinch your little birdie head off," Aggy threatened.

"Chillax, Aggy," Scooter said. "He just needs a minute to settle into his new bod."

"And a muffin. I need a muffin," the bird rattled.

David laughed and Aggy glared at him. "Look, just get the thing a fucking muffin if that's what he wants. It's easier than torturing him."

Aggy tried to think of ways to torture the bird, but finally admitted David was probably right.

Scooter looked at the bird "He did ask politely, and if it keeps him happy and answering questions... You get more flies with honey than vinegar."

"You get even more with shit." Aggy was tired of this already. "By all means get the damn thing a muffin." She didn't really know what their next step was going to be, but knew they couldn't even think to make it without more information. "You're the pot king, stoners get the munchies, and surely you know where to get a muffin."

"There's probably some in the cafeteria. Hell, there may even be some in the vending machine," David said.

"No," the bird said sternly. "I want Mama's muffins."

"Oh you're fucking kidding me," Aggy said. "Why can't they be just any muffins?"

"Because those have toxins and chemicals and too much corn syrup also they won't help me stay regular," Doobie said.

"Fuck, Kirstie got into the alien's head man," Scooter said, as if his mind hadn't already been blown millions of times.

"Scooter, why don't you and David drive back to your son's house, pick up a bunch of those muffins and check on your grandson? On your way back stop and get a pizza."

"Are you sure you mean pizza, Aggy?" David asked. "Are you sure you don't mean anything else?"

"I don't care what you bring back as long as I neither have to go after it, pay for it, nor clean up after you two shit heads."

She watched as they left the lab and turned back to the bird. "Alright you dumb fuck it's just you and me now..."

"And all those things..." It pointed with a wing to the rats. "...and my fellows in their containers."

Aggy grinned and went and got one of the closed containers of Weirdough. She opened the lid and held it over the tank.

"What... What are you doing?" Doobie asked.

"Dumping one of your brothers into the tank. You can answer my questions or watch him die." She dumped the container into the tank and put the lid on.

The bird shrugged its wings. "I never liked him anyway. He was an asshole."

Aggy grabbed another container and dumped it in the tank.

The bird laughed—and here was the thing because it had a parrot's vocal system it sounded like a parrot talking. "I flat hated that bastard. I don't care, more muffins for me."

Damn you David Pratt! I was perfectly happy working in my own little university lab, developing my green stuff, trying to save the planet on my own terms. Sure, I wasn't getting rich on grant money, but I keep a roof over my head, food in my gut, and gas in my hybrid car—and I can sleep at night knowing I'm at least trying to make the world a better place. You blow in, wailing about some crazy crap and now I'm up to my eyeballs in Weirdough and their alien conspiracy to take over the world.

"You seem pensive," Doobie said.

Aggy sighed. "They are getting your muffins. Could you maybe answer one question for me?"

"Promise you won't kill me? You're pretty violent."

"I won't kill you if you answer all my questions. If you don't or if you screw with me, lie to me and make things worse, or if I find out you have lied to me at any point I will pop your head off like a bad zit."

"Fair enough. One question until I get my muffin."

"You little green bastard."

"Mama said when you say a bad word you have to put a nickel in the swear jar."

"You said it."

"So I did; my bad."

"How did you learn English?"

"It's easy. I learned a little while the boy was playing with the Weirdough. When I took over the boy he was still in there with me and when someone spoke to him there was a picture in his head. After I learned basic English it was easy as watching PBS. I also know a bit of Spanish."

It made perfect sense. "The presence that is in there with

you...."

"You mean the soul?"

"You know I'm not going to call it that, smart ass. The presence, is it freaking out?"

"I don't know what you mean."

"Are they scared, unhappy?"

"I only agreed to answer one question before muffin."

"Come on turd it's a two-part question."

"It isn't. This question has nothing to do with the first."

"I'm arguing semantics with a bird. Somebody shoot me," Aggy mumbled. She glared at the bird. "Just answer my question."

"Or you'll what... put more of my enemies into the tank to die? Oh please don't do that."

"I could pull your feathers out one by one."

"That would hurt wouldn't it?"

"Yes, yes it would."

"I'm not a fan of pain. Who hurt you as a child, what's wrong with you?"

"Answer my question."

"They stay in the place they go when they are asleep."

"So they exist in the dream scape?"

"That's another question."

Aggy had forgotten about the Weirdough in the tanks. There was a slight noise and she turned around. In the tank they were just starting to pulse and then they ran right into each other. It was obvious each was trying to possess the other one. In minutes one blinked out. The other stopped pulsing for a minute, came to its full light, and then it rolled around franticly looking for another host till a few seconds later it was gone, too.

"See?" said the bird. "I told you they were assholes."

As they were driving toward Alex's house Scooter was talking on his cell phone, "That's right son, those muffins like Kristie makes... Kirstie then. Why'd you have to marry someone with such a yuppie-assed name? I'm surprised you didn't spell Blake with a Q or a silent seven... She's out of muffins. Man I really need one..."

"I need one, too. Aggy's all-pizza diet is doing a number on my digestive tract."

"I need two... no, no not a dozen... Yeah I suppose it is

just as easy to make a whole batch." Scooter rolled his eyes. "Thanks, we'll be there in a few minutes."

Scooter shut off his phone and glared at David. "Dammit she's making two dozen of them. She's going to think I like the fucking things and I'll have to smile and eat them from now on... You know dude I don't know if it's worth it to save the world."

David laughed and looked out the window. The town had changed a lot but most of the old landmarks were still there. Even with all the weird crap that was going on he had a feeling of nostalgia he couldn't deny and felt more like he was home than he had in years. "Colorado is so pretty."

"Yep and pot is legal so it's just a little slice of heaven on earth. So she ain't here now, what's it like seeing Aggy again?"

"She looks great."

"Dude, that ain't what I'm talking about. How does it feel to see her again?"

David shrugged, "Fine, it's good I guess."

Scooter cut him a look.

David took in a deep breath and let it out. "Alright, it's weird. Okay? I mean, she's changed in a lot of ways, but in just as many she hasn't changed at all. We seem to be unable to talk about our past at all unless we happen to just slip when we get mad at each other and just spit out something we both know shouldn't have been said and doesn't help at all."

"I've been in love dozens of times. It's not rocket surgery. I know love when I see it."

"Scooter I think you may be confusing sex for love."

He laughed. "Ain't no doubt I like me some sex, but I know the difference between love and sex. Now you see dude, I'm like a rooster. I can love me all kinds of hens. But you my friend are like the majestic Alaskan Puffin who mates for life. Aggy and I are tight; she's had a few boyfriends but nothing the least bit serious. You and Aggy are soulmates, man. You belong together."

"Ah come on you don't really believe..."

"Did you ever find another woman you cared even half as much about?"

"I was married."

"And how'd that work out for ya? It didn't last, did it? Why? Because you were never finished with Aggy. She got attacked and you guys never dealt with it the way you still aren't. Man what a woman needs is for a man to be sensitive to her needs. You have to be strong when they need you to be strong but not afraid to show your feelings. They need to know they can talk to you about everything. You have to listen when they're talking—or at least get really good at pretending to. Your problem is you are neither a brute, nor one of those prancing things they call metrosexuals. You're just a normal guy. Normal folks... well how do you handle something like what happened to Aggy? By just not talking about it. Pretending it didn't happen."

"I'd feel more comfortable if she would start the conversation."

"Yes because that worked oh so well twenty years ago. You can't keep laughing it off and avoiding the subject. You have to let yourself feel feelings, bro. Quit shoving them down."

"That's pretty deep, Scooter."

"Yeah, well, I'm like that. I did a lot of things I wasn't very proud of. You know that illegal shit. The drugs I used to sell they screwed people up. My only defense is I was taking them, too, and I wasn't thinking right. They screwed me up, too. When I got clean..."

"You still smoke pot like a chimney."

"Do not, that's bad for you. I eat it now. Pot isn't the same as all that other shit; you know that. I used to be a bad dude. I didn't like me. You have to go in and fix yourself you start to see the truth in things."

"Let's say you're right. Do you really think the middle of an alien invasion is a good time for Aggy and me to have a deep, meaningful conversation about the distant past?"

"Here's what I know about this great big mystery we call life. If you wait for a good time to do things you never get a damn thing done."

David grinned. "Did you read that in a book?"

"A fortune cookie, actually."

"You expect me to act on the words of a fortune cookie?"

"Hey, a fortune cookie made me everything I am today."

"A fortune cookie told you to grow and sell pot?"

"No it said do what you love and you'll always feel rich."

"I don't know where to start, Scooter. If I push her... well she seems to go from zero to pissed off in like five seconds."

"And so do you. You're just going to keep getting on each

other's last nerve until you deal with the giant dead relationship elephant in the room," Scooter said.

"Dude, seriously every relationship you have ever had has ended."

"Harsh and untrue. I'm still friends with all of my old flames... most... well some... a few. Besides I'm a rooster, and you're a ..."

"...Majestic Puffin. Yes, I heard it the first time you said it. She's sort of bitchy right now."

"Really? Dude you just showed up out of the blue after poking her a couple of times on Facebook and laid a huge alien turd in her lap. If situations were reversed how would you take it? And between you and me I haven't noticed she's any bitchier than you are right now. As long as all the past crap is hanging between you, you're just going to keep getting on each other's nerves. You need to clear the air."

"She's snapped at you, too."

"That's the way she and I communicate, dude. I'm annoying; I know I'm annoying, and this is a stressful situation. I'm always flapping my jaw; saying stupid shit. She's stressed out, I don't take it personally. You're a smart dude, quit acting like a dumbass. Quit saying things you know are going to piss her off and then acting surprised when she is. If I were you I'd have some weed mellow out and just let the thoughts flow through me."

"You think pot is the answer to everything."

"It's not just me, a lot of folks do." He pulled into Alex's drive way. "That's how I got filthy rich." He turned the car off and turned to face David. "One of us has a bunch of kids and women who love him everywhere and more money than he can spend and the other just got fired by his alien overlords. Now I don't want to say this but it's clear that while you may have a doctorate I'm a damn sight smarter than you are."

Scooter got out of the car, not letting David address what he'd just said, and when David had a few seconds to think about it he mumbled, "Damn if the hippie bastard isn't right."

CHAPTER NINE

Road Trip

The parrot/alien was ringing that damn bell again. David was stuck sitting beside the thing as Aggy was in the front seat—some excuse about needing to have her computer plugged into the cigarette lighter which frankly he thought was just an excuse because she didn't want to sit next to the bird. There was nowhere else to sit because the entire back seat and back of the van was loaded with crap Scooter or Aggy thought they might need. David still had only the one suitcase he'd showed up with at Aggy's, and half the clothes in it were dirty. Aggy insisted they didn't have time to run a load of clothes and then... Well Scooter spent an hour at his place loading anything he thought might be useful. Then they went to the lab where Aggy spent another hour loading everything she thought they might need. When David said he was pretty sure they had plenty of time to do a load of clothes Aggy told him he should have done them the night before and to shut up.

She had seemed pretty jumpy the entire time they'd been at the university. Something about loading thousands of dollars' worth of university equipment she didn't fill out reams of paper to get permission to take off college property into a psychedelic van with a pot leaf and stoner on the side seemed to make her a little nervous. Not that there was even a moment when she considered she maybe shouldn't do it.

Now they were on the road, the whole back of the van was full, and he was sharing a seat with the bird/alien which was every bit as bad as you would think it might be.

"If you don't stop ringing that fucking bell I'm going to stuff it up your little birdie ass," David snapped.

"I think that would be impossible," Doobie said.

"That won't stop us trying," Scooter said. So apparently he was tired of the bell, too.

"Why are you ringing the bell anyway?" Aggy asked curiously. She was doing something on her computer so maybe she really did need it to be plugged in.

"It's pretty. I like the sound."

"I like the sound that's made when you shut the fuck up and quit ringing the bell," David grated out.

"Hey genius just take the fucking bell away from the wretched thing," Aggy said, her fingers running across the keys on her lap top. He had no idea what she was doing. David hated to admit it but he didn't want to stick his hand in the cage with the possessed bird. As if reading his mind, Aggy set her lap top in the floorboards, twisted into a near impossible position, opened the cage, reached in and yanked the bell out.

"Aw," the parrot said. "You're so mean. Can I have another muffin?"

Aggy locked the door again then looked at David expectantly.

"What?" David asked.

"Can you give it another fucking muffin?"

"Give me a fucking muffin. I want a fucking muffin!" the parrot screeched.

"Oh someone owes a nickel to the swear jar," Aggy said, then she turned around picked her lap top up and went back to work.

"Do not use my words against me! Do not mock me!"

"Here." David stuffed one of the muffins through the bars of the cage cutting it into little box-shaped pieces as it slid through.

"If he keeps eating those like that he's going to shit himself to death," David said. He should know—he had eaten one of the nasty-assed things and taken his first crap in three days.

"You've made a horrid mess of my muffin human," Doobie complained with a mouth full of the stuff.

"Shut your beak hole or we will tape your mouth shut."

"Oh that's a good idea," Aggy said.

"Ahh," the parrot said again, and was silent.

They had questioned the parrot for two days and a dozen muffins. They knew a lot more than they had. Perhaps the most important piece of information was that none of the aliens had one ounce of loyalty to one another. Unfortunately this had Aggy doing Weirdough tank matches for most of those two days. She was bound and determined not to leave any of them alive in her lab. She had made some stupid-assed excuse for the dean about having to make a trip to collect samples for her project which... Well it was a good thing the dean and the rest of the faculty didn't know anything about what Aggy's project really was or they would have known she could get most of what she needed from a nearby cattle ranch and the local feed store.

For David, the best information they had gotten from "Doobie" was that all of the souls that had come to their world to possess their children had been assholes in life. Their religion said that after death the soul went to a good place if you were good and a bad place if you were bad. When the planet started to become toxic and the machine to remove their... presences... was made, only assholes jumped in to be transformed into light and stuck in air-tight jars.

"Why air tight?" Aggy had asked.

"Because the soul..."

"Presence," she corrected

"The soul," the bird went on, "wants to go back to source or into a body. It won't just float around; it always needs to be doing something. Weirdough is the perfect vehicle because it holds us and allows us to interact with the hosts a little but if it gets dry we have to leave it."

So, that was the reason for the warning on the label and in the commercial. "Doobie" told them the plan was for them all to take over hosts at the same time. They were apparently told this while they were still in their jars. Why had so many kids already been affected? Surprisingly when David had asked it was Scooter that answered.

"Dude, kids never put their shit away. Doesn't matter how many times you tell them not to leave that crap out or it will destroy it some kids are still going to do it. Most parents these days don't pick up after their kids. They let them trash everything then bitch that everything is ruined and a mess."

"I didn't have a choice," Doobie said.

"Yes you did. You could have said it was wrong to take over another species and just died," Aggy said.

"But... I'm a narcissistic asshole. Surely you people know I can't think anyone or anything is as important as I am," Doobie said. "And of course I can easily blame anything I do wrong on another."

"I find his honesty refreshing," Scooter said. When David and Aggy turned to look at him like he had lost what was left of his mind he said, "Seriously, most narcissistic assholes never admit there is anything wrong with them."

Doobie stuck the tip of his wing to his beak. "Of course I might be a sociopath. I'm not sure what the difference is."

"There really isn't one," Aggy said.

"So the assholes put their souls into suspended animation till they could find a body to steal. What happened to the good ones?" David asked.

"Oh, they think they are *so* selfless. 'We can't impose ourselves on others, it's not fair.' Boo hoo, what a bunch of quitters! They were all about staying and trying to save the planet. They probably all died in horrible ways and went to their great reward. I didn't care; good people are so judgmental. This is evil and that is evil. There is just no pleasing them unless you're nice and... Well we didn't actually ask them. After all I did say we're all assholes. I am correct that's what you call bad people?"

"So you were never concerned at all with saving your entire race? You allowed millions to die..."

Doobie interrupted David, "*Maybe* die."

"While you go on at any cost?" David was disgusted.

"What do you not understand about we're all narcissistic assholes?"

"How did you discover that you could separate your presence from your body?"

"I believe you people call it transcendental meditation."

"This gets better and better," Aggy muttered, but kept doing what she was doing.

"How does the machine work?"

"I don't understand your question."

"What sort of technology allows you to vacuum pack your presence and ship it across space?" David asked.

"I have no idea how the soul-evicting machine works. The planet was dying. You got in the machine and let them suck your soul out or stayed and died with all the goody-goodies. Then they got to go someplace nice while you went some place bad. Not much of a choice."

"So... someone had to crew the ship that brought you here. Someone had to set up the whole Weirdough scam. Who is running the show?"

"It's assholes, mostly. The good ones helped make the machine and the space ship because they had hope that we would go across the universe, inhabit some small barely-sentient animal, change our attitudes and mend our evil ways. What a bunch of saps! We assholes don't want to change; we're perfectly happy being who we are."

"Who is running things here now?" David asked again.

"There were a dozen of us that kept our original form so that they could pilot the ship and set us up with a base when we found a suitable planet. Even spending long periods of time in suspended animation they were super old by the time we landed. So they captured some of your people and brought them back to the ship and tried to use the machine to get into them but... Adults they weren't able to take over. The personalities were already riveted to the soul, but kids haven't really built an ego yet. They took over some kids and then spent the time their bodies were growing to figure out everything they needed to know about your planet."

David asked the question he really didn't want to ask. "Have you done this before?"

"Of course," answered Doobie. "They used to bottle up convicts and send them across space. The goody-goodies thought that was punishment. You know it wasn't killing them and maybe they'd land somewhere and find suitable hosts and maybe not. I imagine there are several worlds we have taken over by now. It's not like we run around shouting, 'Hello! Alien soul invasion here! Turn over your planet!' We'll most likely stay here till this planet starts to become toxic, at which point we'll find another planet to go to and leave this one to die in peace."

"So you proudly ruin everything you touch."

"We're no different than you," the bird asserted.

"We are *so* different from you, you evil little fucker." David snarled.

"Oh really? You're a planet full of assholes. You trash out, pollute and kill everything. YOU proudly burn up your resources in the process each trying to burn your own hole in the ozone. Hell, a spaceship full of alien assholes shouldn't have any trouble fitting in here at all."

Scooter shook his head. "Dude, he's sort of right."

David ignored Scooter, turning away from the bird. If he kept talking to the creepy-assed thing he'd reach in and strangle it with his bare hands. Then where would they get more information? He took a deep breath to center himself.

"Don't you have a leader? Isn't one of the twelve in control?"

"Certainly."

"I suppose just asking you who it is would be too simple."

"Well duh! I could say I'm the leader, being the best and brightest of my kind, if I do say so myself. But then you have to figure in the asshole factor because all the others think that they should be the leader too. If you go far enough up the ladder, as it were, you'd eventually find the head asshole."

"What's its name?"

"Hell I don't know."

"How can you not know?"

"I don't care who runs the show as long I don't have to. There are two kinds of assholes—ones that want to be in charge and boss people around and ones who are happy to let the other kind bust their ass while they coast through life."

"But Weirdough, Inc. is a huge company, how are you keeping the humans at the top from figuring out what you're doing?"

"You're kidding me right? The humans at the top of Weirdough all know what we're doing."

"Why are you waiting? Why aren't you all just jumping right into kids?"

"That would be a huge mistake. Look at how fast you caught on. Stupid human children leave us out of the containers. We can die or jump the gun and take over the kids. We're supposed to take them over all at once. We're supposed to just die if they leave us out early, but... You can't expect such selfless behavior of assholes."

"How the hell are you going to take all the kids over at once?"

"We're still waiting for some clown to get his act together. Really the problem with being so dependent on humans is that you're all so very incompetent."

"How is it possible that humans are willingly helping you take over the bodies of children?" Why on earth would they go along with your crazy plan for world domination? After all, they've got to live here, too."

"No they don't. Rich people don't live in the same world everyone else does. What's going to happen to them if they help us? They are going to get even richer. Let's face it; they are assholes just like us. Just powerful meat suits revved up and ready to do whatever we say to make a buck. I don't know why your kind assumes that knowledge is equal to power. The top executives are very aware of exactly what we are and what we're doing and they *simply don't care*. Funny how easy it is to get what you want when you offer a lot of money and the power that goes with it. Pretty simple as far as plans go."

"Okay, so these people are willing selling out the human race."

"Uncle Toms, man," Scooter said.

"Come on, David, like you didn't know corporate America is corrupt. Hell if you really think about it, helping Aliens take over the world... it's not even the worst thing they did this *week*," Aggy said.

"You things sure have a lot of rules and regulations that were a waste of our time. Your kind sure loves red tape. We needed someone to work the kinks out and the rich guys were happy to help. So much unnecessary bullshit, so many hoops to jump through. You whine about me poking a little bell! At least it makes a pretty sound that makes me happy."

"Get to the point bird."

"In your system there are permits and inspections and requirements, property to be purchased and prepared, supplies to get and so on and so on. We figured out who could be bought. We didn't even have to buy you. We just told you what we needed and you developed the formula for the soul-holding transporting Weirdough compound."

"Are there factories loading up Weirdough with alien presences all over the world?" Aggy had asked.

"No just the one, but we're planning to ship worldwide."

"Beautiful," Aggy intoned.

"You sound so confident," David said "How can you be so sure that humanity won't catch on? We figured it out, and we have every intention of putting your little invasion to a halt."

"Look who's confident now!" squawked the bird.

"Not confident. *Determined*." David had to admit that he felt a little silly arguing with a bird even if it really wasn't. "You don't understand true human nature at all. You're just... an alien thing stuck in a bird."

"You keep referring to my present state as one that should be unsatisfactory. I like this body. Perhaps you'd be a little more self-assured if you were in a different body."

David looked over at the bird happily devouring his muffin and had a sobering thought. "Would your machine work on humans? In other words can a person be moved from their body to some sort of storage? If someone had a disease or injury there's no cure or fix for, could we store our consciousness temporarily until an empty vessel—so to speak—could be found?"

"What sort of empty vessel, David?" Aggy asked. From her tone she obviously didn't like the direction she thought he was going in.

David shrugged. "I don't know maybe a cloned body of some kind or maybe parrots..."

"Hardly seems fair to the parrots," Scooter disapproved.

"Cloned parrots maybe," David defended.

"Don't be silly. Even if our technology would work on you, we would certainly never share it with you," Doobie said.

"Why the hell not?"

"I told you we are assholes. Why do you need any other explanation? Perhaps I don't understand the definition of asshole properly."

"Nope you've got it. You definitely are one," Aggy muttered

The bird turned to David and gave him a smug look. "There would be nothing that could be gained from us sharing our technology with you."

"You selfish little bastard! After all the muffins I fed you. All the times I've wanted to strangle you and didn't. There's gratitude for you." David didn't know why this was making him so mad. It wasn't like he was sick or had a sick loved one he wanted to save. Maybe he just didn't like having the thing mock him. As if knowing he was getting on David's last nerve and wanting to finish strong, the damn thing started to laugh at him.

"Aw, did I hurt your feelings? You poor baby! How did you make it this long as a species when you are all so clueless?"

Being unable to come up with a snappy come back, David hit the cage hard with his elbow knocking the bird off the perch he'd been sitting on.

"Hey you did that on purpose," Doobie complained as he righted himself. "Stupid humans!"

"You are being a real douche bag, Doobie," Scooter scolded. "Let me tell you something you smug fuckers didn't take into account when you made your really great plan. You can get away with damn near anything with the common man except fucking with his kids. You go after people's kids they are going to hunt you till they find you and then they are going to string you up by your glowing soul balls."

David turned in his seat away from the bird. He leaned up to peer over Aggy's shoulder trying to see what she was doing on her laptop. Mostly he was trying to see if she was really working or playing some online game only pretending to work. "What are you working on? It's about time for a seat switch. I'm getting sick to my stomach."

"Yes, because you always do when you no longer want to sit in the back seat," Aggy replied. "I finally got a floor plan for the factory from city hall files and now I'm in the middle of downloads. I'm going to be here a bit. The security firewall was a bitch to hack through. I must have been a pirate in a former life, just not quite the same kind of pirate." She grinned and held a hand over one eye to mimic an eyepatch, the other hand she'd crooked her finger into a hook and made a swiping motion at him with it. "Avast, ye scurvy alien assholes! I be boardin' your computer files! Take no prisoners!"

"Glad to see you're having such a good time, Aggy. I don't think you will think it's so funny when I'm hurling all over the car," David said in a monotone.

"Knock yourself out. I mostly deal with shit all day. As you know I don't have a weak stomach. If you really get sick just puke in the bird's cage," Aggy said. She went back to ignoring him.

David looked over at the bird.

"Don't you dare," Doobie said, swiveling his head to glare at David.

"How about you, Scooter? You need a break? Want me to drive for a while?"

"No man, I'm good. I usually run on a couple hours of sleep anyway. I like to drive."

David sighed and resigned himself to sitting in the back seat next to the parrot. He thought seriously about starting to bitch that he needed to pee but decided he should wait until he actually had to go. He tried to take a nap in an attempt to avoid dealing with the possessed green thug he shared a seat with and was almost asleep when he was startled awake with the words...

"Go to sleep David, that's right," crooned Doobie softly. "Go to sleep."

"Gah!" David yelped and grabbed the jacket he'd been using for a pillow. He scooted as far away from the cage as he could. "Keep your little feathered ass as far away from me as possible! And stop singing! It's creepy."

Scooter peered in the back seat. "Am I gonna have to separate you two?"

"Very funny," said David. "Just wait until he starts singing to *you*."

"Shut your seed-hole bird," Aggy said, not looking away from her computer.

"He asked me questions. You ordered me to answer questions."

"He wasn't asking you a question when you started to torment him. Shut the fuck up and leave him alone or I'll … poke you with a sharp stick," Aggy said.

"Do you have a sharp stick?"

"I could get a sharp stick you little green dumbass."

"You have a definite mean streak," Doobie accused Aggy.

"I do, so shut up!"

The bird shut up and David found he actually felt warm that Aggy would come to his defense against the bird.

David must have gone to sleep because when he opened his eyes they were at a gas station. He looked down and Aggy had hold of his knee she had obviously been shaking him to wake him up. He nodded, silently slapped his leg till it woke up then got out of the van. He looked at where Scooter was already putting gas in the vehicle.

"Do you need help?"

"Nope I got it. Go on in and drain your lizard."

Still half asleep, feeling off balance and brain fogged he stepped through the front doors and almost ran smack dab into Aggy who had stopped just inside the door. He followed her gaze and didn't have to ask what she was looking at. There was a TV playing in the corner and Pork Chop the Weirdough Clown was on the screen.

"…That's right boys and girls. Keep watching! Coming up very soon we will give you instructions and you will all get the thrill of your lives. Weirdough isn't just any toy, no it's the best toy in the whole world, but it's going to get even better. Just you wait and see."

The commercial ended. David and Aggy looked at each other and together said, "That can't be good."

CHAPTER TEN

It All Comes Out in the End

He didn't know whether it was the bird's muffin he had eaten or the fact that he had bought a bottle of fruit juice and a yogurt at every gas station quick pick they had stopped at along the way, but he finally felt like he could go, in that "it had better be soon" way. When Scooter parked in the drive way of David's house in Overland Park, David jumped out, ran to the front door opened it and sprinted to his bathroom. It wasn't till he flipped the lights on and sat down that he saw that the room had been tossed. His stuff had been thrown everywhere in a way that said whoever did it was looking for something. It didn't matter—he had more pressing things to deal with first.

David finished, flushed, washed his hands and walked out of the bathroom leaving the light on. Walking down the hall he could see that the lights in the living room were on. When he walked into the room Scooter and Aggy were standing just inside the door looking around. If anything the living room looked worse than the bathroom. Scooter looked a little shocked but Aggy looked down right smug.

"Why David, I just love what you've done with the place! Seriously, you have some nerve to bitch about the way I keep house."

"Yeah, man," Scooter said. "I've got all kinds of kids and grandkids tripping through my place spilling crap I didn't know I had and it doesn't look this bad."

"It's not bad housekeeping, you morons! I've obviously been robbed! Do you honestly think I'd leave my house like this?"

"You did leave suddenly," Aggy pointed out with a shrug.

"Seriously? Do you think I could do this much damage packing? Someone has ransacked this house. I've got to see what's been taken."

"Should we call the police?" Aggy asked.

"No cops, man, no cops," Scooter said, flapping his arms

around in the air like he was beating off mosquitos.

"Scooter's right; it might be the aliens," David said. "I've got to see what—if anything—has been taken. Everybody pick a room and we'll split up and search."

"Since we aren't Mystery, Inc. and we don't have a big talking dog I suggest we don't split up and look for clues. I think we should stay together. Besides how would Scooter and I have any idea if anything has been taken when we don't know what the hell you had in the first place?" She lowered her voice. "What if they're still here?"

"Whoever was here is surely long gone by now."

David waded in to search the front room. Piles of foam leaked from slashed sofa cushions and shattered glass covered the floor. The couch lay on its side, the bottom and arms cut open and stuffing yanked out and tossed around the room. Books had been thrown around, pages torn and scattered. The television had been torn off its wall mount and had a large stomp mark crackling the glass. Shelves had been overturned as well as the coffee table. They'd even broken the frame holding his degree. They weren't just looking for something they were obviously making it personal, but as far as he could tell they hadn't taken anything.

Aggy followed David into the kitchen and when David saw she had pulled her gun and was holding it in both fists scanning the room, far from being annoyed he was relieved.

Aggy used the barrel of the gun to open the cabinets. She was pretending to help but was in fact mostly looking for something to drink, preferably rum. *Those fucking hateful alien bastards have broken every bottle of booze.* "Vindictive little shits." She muttered. *They must have been really pissed when they couldn't find anything. Well, the bird did say they were all assholes.*

Scooter poked his head in the kitchen and saw the mess. "I hate to sound like a chicken shit, but I'm going to go sit in the van with Doobie. Not like he'd drive off on his own, but..." He trailed off.

"Good idea," Aggy said. "That bird would give us up in a heartbeat."

"They must know I took stuff on the flash drive. They must know we are on to them."

"And how would they know that, David? Now is not the

time to be overly paranoid. There is enough real stuff to worry about. All they know is that you asked a lot of questions that made them uncomfortable, and that you knew about the problem with the product. They were probably watching your house to see if you were going to alert the authorities. When they realized you had left and not come back they most likely tossed the place looking for clues about where you were. I'm sorry about your house and your stuff David, but we need to get the hell out of here in case they're still watching the house. Do you need help gathering your clothes? Anything you want to take with you?" asked Aggy.

David covered his face with his hands for a moment then dropped them and turned and looked at Aggy. "You know what? We're driving around with a hippie bazillionaire. He can buy me new clothes. Let's just get the hell out of here."

Aggy kept her gun in hand and they beat a hasty retreat from the house. David purposely sat in the front seat, forcing Aggy to sit in the back with the bird. Not too surprisingly Scooter already had the van running and even as the words, "Go, go, go," left Aggy's mouth Scooter was already backing out of the drive way.

They hadn't gone far when Scooter said, "Bigger than shit we've got a tail." He sped up. He took a corner without slowing, and for a minute Aggy was sure the van was going to go right over. It handled like a cow in a wind tunnel.

She looked out the back window but couldn't see a damn thing because of course they had packed the back of the van till there was only three inches of open window at the top. She'd shoot at them but the side window didn't open.

"How many of them are in the car?" Aggy asked.

"One," Scooter said.

"Can you lose him?" David asked.

"Maybe. I don't know," Scooter said.

Aggy's mind was working fast. It was only a matter of time till either the alien caught them or a cop pulled them over. They couldn't afford a car chase through most of the city; that only worked on TV cop dramas.

"Slam the brakes on. Let him close the gap and then slam the brakes." As Aggy said it she put on her seat belt.

"Wait, wait!" David yelled. "That's your plan, let him hit us?"

"He ain't gonna hurt this van," Scooter said, and then he

hit the brakes.

"Brace for impact," squawked the bird. "Brace for impact!"

"Fuck!" David yelled.

Then there was the crunch of metal. Aggy's whole body was thrown against the seat belt and the bird—cage and all—fell with a crash into the floor. Aggy might have been hurt, but she didn't have time to worry about it as she pulled off her seat belt, opened the door and jumped out of the car. She ran back to threaten and maybe question the alien, but her plan had worked a little too well. The alien's human brain was soup across the wind shield. *He should have been wearing a seat belt,* she thought, turned quickly to run back to the van and literally ran into David. There was a moment when they were both startled.

"He's dead," Aggy announced.

"We need to check him make sure he doesn't have pictures on his cell phone or a camera," David said. "They already know what I look like. I've got it; you get in the van."

She got in and a few seconds later David climbed in and shut the door. Without a word being uttered Scooter raced off. She guessed he had enough of a view in his rear view mirror to know what happened.

It was only when Aggy was settled back into her seat that she realized what David had done. She smiled. *He had my back. He followed me not knowing what I might be doing to help me do whatever it was.*

"What now?" David asked, taking a cell phone from his pocket. He made sure it was off.

Aggy thought that was a good question.

"How about for starters someone picks my cage up off the floor? It smells funny down here, like pot and desperation. I can't see anything."

Aggy picked the cage back up and righted it in the seat next to her.

"Why don't I have a seat belt? I should have a seat belt! Is no one concerned at all about my safety?"

"Shut up bird," Aggy ordered. "We just killed someone!"

"Not on purpose, and it was some alien slime ball who stole a kid's body twenty some years ago," Scooter was quick to point out.

David was obviously losing whatever was left of his cool, and Aggy couldn't blame him because so was she.

"No one's going to care that we didn't kill him on purpose, just that he's dead and we are fleeing the scene of the accident," he said.

"But we are all clear—I didn't kill him we all did," Scooter said. "Just so we're all clear on that."

"Yes, Scooter, it was my idea; I'm not going to blame you. What the hell do we do now?" Aggy asked, borrowing David's original question with at least as much intensity.

"I don't know why you're all shook up now," the bird said to Aggy. "You have been killing my people for days. Oh I get it. It's the flesh bag he was wrapped in that bugs you."

"I said shut up bird!" Aggy pointed her gun at him, and he was silent.

"Aggy put the gun away now," Scooter said in an amazingly calm voice. "Let's all just take a step back and calm down. Take a deep breath and find our centers. Breath in slowly, fill your diaphragm..."

"Are you fucking kidding us now, Scooter?!" Aggy yelled.

"That is not calm, Aggy. Take a deep breath in fill your belly and then drop it with the sound *hee*."

"Scooter I swear to God..." David started.

"You too, David, calm deep breath in and drop it with the sound *hee*."

David she was sure did it for the same reason he did—just to shut Scooter up. But surprisingly after he had done it three times he did feel calmer and then...

Well then Scooter very calmly said, "I have some friends that own a body shop. I texted them as soon as the car hit us when I accidentally—not on purpose at all—stopped short. They are on their way to open up for us even as we speak. They'll trade out the rear bumper and give us a new paint job. While they are working on the van one of them will run us to a hotel where we will get cleaned up, watch some tube and relax."

David was only half listening to the conversation. He kept thinking about his house. Mostly he kept thinking about how he had pulled his friends into this nightmare. And about all the sticky stuff he'd had to pick through to find the guy's phone.

"...We need a pet-friendly hotel. Something high end, though 'cause we've had a hell of a day," Scooter said.

"Anything for you, Scooter." The kid from the body shop that was driving them looked at Scooter with only slightly less admiration than he might have for a rock star. "Your shit changed my grandma's life! She moved to Colorado when they made pot legal. She had glaucoma; couldn't see shit. Now she feels fine, no pressure or pain in her eyes at all, and I have to tell you she's a damn sight easier to get along with. Granny says your shops have the best product at an affordable price."

"Give me her name and tell me which of my shops she frequents before we leave tomorrow and I'll be sure granny gets a huge discount on her weed."

The kid thanked him then made sure he had Scooter's cell phone number. "I'll call you in the morning as soon as we're done with the van."

When they got to the shop, Scooter and Aggy had made a quick check of the equipment they had in the back. Aggy sighed and said her centrifuge was damaged. "I can probably just blame it on an explosion in the lab."

At which point Scooter muttered, "Another couple inches of impact and it wouldn't have been the only thing that exploded."

The shop's boss—an old friend from Scooter's distant and not so legal past—had assured Scooter he'd make the van a priority job and have it ready the next day, new paint and all, no questions asked.

David couldn't get the image of the guy smashed all over the inside of his car out of his head. And his house, the house he had lived in, torn completely to shreds. Were they going to jail? Were they going to be killed by aliens?

When they arrived at the hotel Aggy looked up at it and wondered if it was such a good idea to stay at the most expensive hotel in town, but she couldn't think of any reason the aliens could find them easier there than at some rat trap. She was tired, stressed completely out, and felt like she deserved to have a nice comfy clean bed bug free room. God knew that would make it a lot different from home.

Scooter went to get them checked in while Aggy waited with David in the lobby. She could tell by David's posture that he was used to staying in places like this. She really wasn't. She made a living, not much more, and since she hadn't managed to actually develop the product she was always working on—just various degrees of close—she didn't go and lecture at other colleges. She made decent money not great money. Even if she had a little extra she wouldn't have wasted it on something like this but... It wasn't her money and she was going to enjoy it. She just wished they'd hurry up and get them in a room because she was wired for sound and frankly standing there in the wide-open lobby was making her sweat.

"Keep your beak shut, bird. Nobody here needs to hear your yapping," Aggy whispered menacingly.

David watched as the damn thing started to open his mouth, then faked a yawn and shut up.

"Yeah, that's what I'm talking about."

David chuckled then felt bad about his moment of mirth. After all they had just killed a man... of course he wasn't really a man. Maybe the bird was right and the only reason he was more upset about this than all the aliens Aggy had vanquished in the lab is that this one was all wrapped up in a fleshy human bag that had busted and bled all over on impact. *And somewhere in that thing was the child's presence that never got to grow up and... well now he is free to go... wherever such things go if they go anywhere and... it just isn't a very good time to be a scientist.*

A bell boy rolled a cart over, picked up their pathetic luggage and took off without so much as a nod of his head. David looked from himself to Aggy. They looked like what they were—worn out, mostly dirty people whose clothes were wrinkled from a six and a half hour car ride. People who had found their destination ransacked, been chased by an alien wearing a human suit that they had caused to kill itself, and now they were on the run... Well maybe they didn't look exactly like that but it was close and no small wonder the bell boy didn't really want to interact with them.

Aggy chased the bell boy down and stuck the cage on the luggage cart.

When he caught up David asked, "Is that safe?"

"You mean the creepy-assed thing might start talking about exactly what we're doing and what he is and such?"

David nodded.

"Well first I heard the bell boy talking to the concierge and he barely speaks English. Second, who's going to believe the crazy shit that comes out of a bird's mouth? Hell if you and I whipped out copies of our doctorates and spouted the truth no one would believe us."

"Point taken."

Scooter showed up a few seconds later waving three card keys in the air.

They headed straight for the elevator and got on.

David looked down at his watch. It was only nine, but his body was telling him it was at least three in the morning. He looked at his watch again, why? *Because it's the only nice thing I own which hasn't been completely destroyed. My house is in ruins and if I'm honest in this moment I don't really care because that is the least of my problems. It wasn't my intention but I have dragged Aggy and Scooter into something insanely dangerous. And how cowardly am I that I have no problem at all dragging Aggy into this mess, but I can't tell her I'm sorry about how, when, and why I left.*

They were all silent and David realized Aggy and Scooter were as worn out as he was. The elevator didn't stop till they were on the top floor. When the doors opened it was obvious that the whole top flour only had four suites, so David knew before their door opened that the suite was going to be lavish. While he had stayed in five-star hotels before, he'd never actually been in one of the huge suites, and certainly nothing like this.

"Holy shit," Aggy said.

"Yeah." David nodded and he watched as the Bell boy stood with the cart waiting for instructions.

"Just dump 'em, bud. We'll chose up sides and go to bed in a minute."

The bell boy unloaded their bags and the bird.

The huge, bald-bearded hippie gave him a one-hundred-dollar bill and then the bell boy thanked him and pushed his little cart out of the room shutting it behind him.

There was a fully-stocked bar and Aggy beat him to it. She picked up a bottle of rum held it up to her ear and said, "What's that you say, rum? I should drink you... Well okay." She poured herself a tumbler full then headed for the nearest huge overstuffed chair and flopped more than sat on it. She took a long drink then said, "So Scooter, are you married right now?"

"You know I'm not and not lookin' but I'm always open for taking a road trip with friends." He laughed and looked at

David with meaning.

Scooter probably would have given Aggy a tumble long ago if she was really interested and if he didn't think she was cosmically linked to David.

Aggy was already nearly done with the huge drink she'd poured herself. She saw David watching her. "What? I'm not driving anywhere."

David smiled. "But you are armed and very dangerous."

Aggy pulled her gun out from behind her back and held it out. "Here, you take it then."

David sighed went over and took the gun from her, wondering who would protect them if the aliens showed up if Aggy was hell bent on getting sloshed. But she finished her drink, stood up and walked off to find the hot tub Scooter had told her was in the room.

David poured himself a scotch. "You want something, Scooter?" David asked.

"Naw, hard liquor is the tool of the man, bad for yer liver and stuff. It ain't natural and makes you do crazy, unnatural things... Sort of like my third wife Bonnie." He rolled his eyes. "That woman was crazier than a shit house rat, but super good in the sack. Nothing fucks like crazy, and it took me awhile to learn not to stick my dick in crazy."

David took his drink and sat where Aggy had been sitting. He took the alien's cell phone from his pocket. By a stroke of luck—the kind he didn't normally have—the cell phone had been sitting on the hood of the car where it had no doubt flown out the hole the guy's body made. He'd had to pick it up out of a pile of goo he didn't want to think about. Now that he had he went to the bar and used a bar towel to wipe it off and then he washed his hands. He went back and sat down then he turned the phone on to check its contents.

There were no photos that had been sent except of naked women the alien had pulled off the internet. David found that interesting. What did an alien get from looking at naked human women? Then he realized it had a human body so... Probably the same thing David did. The alien's text messages of the last few minutes before his death didn't really tell more than an update that David had returned and had two other humans with him. No descriptions. He turned it off. Maybe Aggy could find something they could use on it later.

Scooter fixed him with a glare.

"What? Does my drinking offend you, Pot King?" David laughed.

Scooter sat down across from him. "Nope I'm offended by what a big wet pussy you are. The universe started an alien invasion just so that you and your soul mate could get back together, and you won't go with her to find that hot tub and get freaky in it."

"Dude I don't know what the hell goes on in what's left of your brain. It's not like some prophecy foretold that a time would come when the chosen ones would fight the great evil and end up naked in a hot tub."

"Oh I see you like her," Doobie said.

David had forgotten all about the damned thing which no doubt was its intention.

"Listen here, bird..."

"I can't imagine why you'd like her. She's very unkempt and mean."

"You better shut your beak bird, shut it right now." David still had Aggy's gun in his hand and he leveled it at the bird. "I will blow your fucking half-witted alien head off."

"Ah come on David this is such a nice clean room." Scooter sighed.

"I'm sensing anger, David," the bird said. "Perhaps you think I have said something I didn't intend. All I said was..." And then he said slowly as if David were an imbecile, "You. Like. Her."

Scooter got up walked over and pried the gun out of David's hand. "Ah, I'll just take this for safe keeping till Aggy is sober again." Then he walked over picked up the cage, walked with it into one of the bedrooms and came out shutting the door behind him a few minutes later without the bird or the gun. He sat back down across from David.

"Now where were we, before we were so rudely interrupted?" Scooter started. "Oh I know! I was explaining what a fucking chicken shit you are."

"It's not that simple, Scooter."

"It is absolutely that simple. Just go find her and talk to her. Quit trying to write just the right speech to present to her and just talk to her from your heart."

"What did you do with the bird?"

"Stuck him in the room I'm taking in front of the TV and gave him a pot-laced brownie to eat... I ate one, too, you know because it was a two pack and I didn't want it to go to waste."

Aggy found the hot tub and took a good, long soak. It seemed to quicken the effects of the rum she drank which suited her just fine. She'd put on one of the hotel robes and walked back into the huge living room to find David sitting watching TV, an empty glass in his hand.

"Where's my gun?" she asked, seeing it nowhere near him.

"Scooter took it. I was threatening the bird with it. Sometimes new Scooter can be such a party pooper." Suddenly riotous laughter erupted from the next room obviously both the bird and Scooter.

"What the..."

"Scooter and the bird got stoned together."

On the TV the commercial came on and there was that hatefully disfigured clown Pork Chop. He seemed to be looking straight at her, and despite all the booze and the twenty-minute hot tub she had just taken, Aggy's blood ran cold.

"It's come to my attention that some boys and girls didn't put their Weirdough away in its container and now they don't have it to play with anymore. Don't be all sad because you lost your Weirdough! Always, always put it away boys and girls. You don't want to be the only children to miss out on the big secret. Keep watching and take care of your Weirdough!"

Laughter erupted from the next room again, and David said quickly, "By the way don't believe everything that parrot says. He's a horrible liar."

"And so is that fucking clown."

CHAPTER ELEVEN

Don't Eat That; You Don't Know Where It's Been

Aggy looked at the cart loaded with food Scooter had ordered from room service.

"Most of the hotels I stay at have the complimentary continental breakfast till about nine—so really before humans should even think about eating. I don't know which continent they come from but apparently coffee there tastes like swill, juice is always warm or gone and someone always screws up the waffle maker by pouring in too much batter and it burns or gets it stuck. If you're lucky you get half a bagel you have to cage fight some other poor sucker for." She swatted David's hand when he reached for the plate in front of her. "Hey, ass hat, leave some for the rest of us."

David grinned at her through a mouth full of bacon and kept loading his plate. So in other words he mostly ignored her.

"I'm hungry, too," said Doobie. "Why am I so hungry? And my mouth feels really dry. Who's got a drink for a thirsty birdie?"

"I didn't know what everyone would want, so I just ordered everything. Everything breakfast that is," Scooter said. He opened the cage and threw a blueberry muffin in for Doobie.

"I could get used to this," Aggy said.

"What?" Gasped David in mock horror. "And give up your beloved all-pizza diet? Say it ain't so Aggy!"

"You're going to wish it wasn't so when I put my boot in your ass," Aggy teased him back.

"I see fruit on your plate! Actual fruit!"

"I hope it doesn't screw up my digestive track," Aggy said. "It's not like I never eat fruit. You can get pineapple on your pizza you know."

"Hello! Doobie wants a drink. Doobie wants a drink!"

"There is water in your dish," Scooter said.

"Mommy always gave me a bendy straw and juice. Where is my juice box you cheap ungrateful bastards...?"

"For the love of God give the screaming thug some juice." Aggy reached in, grabbed his water dish, dumped it then filled it from the bottle of grape juice and put it back in the bird's cage.

"See now was that so difficult?" Doobie said. He took a drink then said, "Yum, grape juice! You aren't allowed to have this on the sofa, it stains."

"Man." Scooter sighed. "It's worse than I thought. The poor little dumplin' don't have a shot! They got rules about everything over there."

The TV was on and almost like it was there just to remind them of what they were doing that damn clown popped up and did an ad.

"Hey boys and girls," Pork chop started. "It sure is good to see so many of you today. Don't forget to put your Weirdough away and keep tuned for the big surprise." Then there was a little song about all the things you could do with Weirdough. "You can stretch it and bend it, not eat it or drink it, you can break it and mend it and even unthink it—but never leave it out of its box..."

"Or it will steal your body and make you eat Lox," David finished. They all laughed—except the bird.

"I fail to see the humor," Doobie said, and went right back to drinking his juice.

"That's because you're a body-stealing alien and an unrepentant asshole."

"I *am* pretty unrepentant."

"Is that clown one of you?" Aggy asked Doobie.

"Are you kidding? None of us would lower ourselves like that," Doobie said.

"So says the alien in the parrot body," David mumbled.

"So the clown is an actual human?" Aggy asked.

"I suppose so. He certainly isn't one of us."

They had taken a cab to pick up the van. When they got there David took one look at the paint job and cringed.

"You guys did an awesome job," Scooter said with real appreciation.

"Nothing's too good for the king."

"Scooter man," David whispered in his ear. "Now the thing is bright yellow with a giant red pot leaf on the side. There is a cartoon of you smoking a doobie with a huge crown made of rolling papers on your head. That's hardly inconspicuous."

"Why does it say 'We support local business'?" Aggy asked.

"We do man. Our bongs are all hand crafted by local artisans," Scooter said. "It's always good to put money back into the community. I like to support the arts."

Aggy looked at David. "It's alright; it works for what we're doing."

And what were they doing? Well Aggy had found out online that Weirdough, Inc. was looking for investors. It hadn't been hard for her to pretend to be Scooter's secretary and set up a meeting with one of the executives with the legendary pot tycoon Scooter Stewart. David had learned in the conversation that led to Aggy calling Weirdough, Inc. that Scooter had legally changed his name years ago and refused to tell anyone what his birth name was. He said it was something too embarrassing and painful to recall which was saying a lot when it came from a guy who used to haul drugs around in his ass.

David still wasn't sure it was a good plan even as he sat in the back seat without the bird. They had left Doobie in their hotel room watching TV and stoned on yet another pot brownie. Not unlike many assholes he mellowed out when he was wasted. David wasn't sure it was a good idea to leave Doobie in the hotel unprotected but had to admit part of him would rather the aliens at Weirdough, Inc. grabbed the bird and found out everything they knew than be stuck in the van with the little green menace.

"I still think I should have come alone," Scooter said.

"No way, Scooter, you need back up," David said.

"Yep, but all I have is you guys." Scooter laughed.

David lay down in the seat way before they reached the destination. He couldn't afford to be seen and since Aggy couldn't take her gun into the building he was their back up.

Scooter parked the van and then got out looking determined in his cargo shorts and over-washed powder blue T shirt. Aggy looked the part in a smart black pants suit, her dark hair tied back in a single pony tail that reached to just past her shoulders. She turned to look at him where he had just slipped from the seat on into the floorboards just to be on the safe side. She grinned at him winked grabbed her tablet and got out of the van.

He had his cell phone in his hand. If they got into trouble they were going to call him and he was going to.... Do what exactly? He really had no idea. So mostly he was just lying there hoping they didn't get into trouble and making up plans that would never in a million years work if they did.

Doesn't seem like a *factory run by a group of evil aliens determined to take over the world* Aggy thought as she declined the receptionist's offer of an espresso or water while she and Scooter waited. The name plate on the woman's desk exclaimed in huge bright yellow letters that she was Janet. *I can't afford to drop my guard. This glorified phone girl might be human or she may be one of them. I'm a scientist. I have to remember things aren't always what they seem and of course it just looks like a normal factory. It's as much a front as their human bodies are. I need to keep my eyes wide open, stay sharp and hope nothing goes wrong.*

"I'll go tell Mister Johnson you're here," Janet said. She stood and left walking down a short hall.

Aggy sat next to Scooter and poked him with her elbow when he started fidgeting. Why? Because Scooter wasn't a fidget; he was way too laid back for that. He was fidgeting because he was nervous and someone like Scooter wouldn't likely be nervous about investing a small part of his vast fortune in a company that was taking in millions a day. The wait wasn't long.

"Right this way," Janet announced a few minutes later as she walked back into the room.

They stood up and followed her down the short hallway and made a left turn before she opened the door to show them in.

Right turn, back up the hallway and out the door—I need to keep track of where we are in case we have to make a run for it. Mostly I need to keep my cool, so I don't give us away thus making sure that we DO have to make a run for it. It's been a long time since I have actually run anywhere; I may not be any good at it.

Janet swung the door wide. "Here they are Mister Johnson." She smiled a broad, sincere smile at them and Aggy found it unnerving.

If they have been living with us, raised in homes with us, there isn't going to be any way at all to tell the aliens from the humans. Everything from their speech patterns to their body language would be just like ours.

Mister Johnson was a tall man with thinning, blondish hair that he wore in a bad comb over. He had a sprayed-on tan, teeth too big for his head and beady eyes. Aggy frowned; he was obviously trying to look like the idiot that stole the presidency and what could that mean? He no doubt looked up to the asshole, but did that mean he was just a super-greedy human willing to sell the human race out to the highest bidder or was he an alien asshole wearing the body he had stolen some thirty years ago?

He stood up behind his desk and smiled a smile so insincere that Aggy was immediately sure he was an alien until she remembered that all corporate executives were lying, crooked, deceitful bastards and she went right back to not knowing.

"Mister Johnson." Scooter walked right over and shook the guy's hand over the desk. "I'm Scooter Stewart; this is my assistant Aggy Jones. Ms. Jones is in charge of our financial division. My accountant and Ms. Jones tell me I need to diversify my stock portfolio. You know, tie up some dough for a bit so I can pay a few million dollars less in taxes." They quit shaking hands and Scooter continued. "I have to say I'm very interested in investing in Weirdough, Inc." Scooter looked at Aggy and Aggy realized she needed to shake the guy's hand too so she did so quickly. Whatever the guy was he gave her the creeps, human or alien he was the enemy.

"To tell the truth, Mister Johnson..."

"Ted." He sat back down.

"Ted, then and you can just call me Scooter. Not even my old man went by Mister Stewart. As I was saying, I'd never heard of your product before my grandson started talking about it and well, anything that keeps that kid's interest longer than it takes yeast to fart must be pretty entertaining."

Mister Johnson laughed and waved at the two huge over-stuffed leather chairs seated in front of his desk. "Make yourselves comfortable. Would you like something to drink?"

"I'm good. What about you, Aggy?"

"I'm fine." She realized she was more nervous than Scooter was and quickly realized why. He was used to dealing with big business assholes, and he had been in the drama department at college as long as she and David had. She had elbowed Scooter and Scooter had slipped into character, a role that was easy for him because he was after all playing himself. She needed to slip into character too or she, not Scooter, was going to blow their cover.

They sat down and Aggy took her tablet from her purse so that she could pretend to be taking notes about the business and could in reality take notes that might help them learn more about the aliens.

"We would be very interested in helping you diversify your stock portfolio, Mister... Scooter."

Aggy checked the man's body language. He was nervous, but nervous like 'I want this guy's money' not 'These guys are on to our alien scheme to take over the world' nervous.

"We are actually looking to expand our business globally, and extra capital would help us in that endeavor. We have had incredible success with our product that could only be helped by expanding our markets and our product line."

I don't like the sound of that, Aggy thought. *Considering their product harbors an alien soul looking to take over a human host in every colorful container. We just went from taking over the country to global domination.*

"Look, as I'm sure Aggy could explain better than I can, whether my investment with you makes money or not doesn't matter a diddly-shit to me," Scooter said.

"Beg pardon?"

Scooter looked at Aggy and Aggy could have kicked him. She wasn't really a financial advisor. Then she remembered one of the many reasons she hated big money and corporations. "Scooter makes a lot of money, Mister Johnson. He's looking for a tax write off."

"I hate the man dude," Scooter explained.

In truth Scooter was the only rich man Aggy had ever known who didn't fudge on his taxes. He said the system worked for him and that since the system worked for the rich they should be more than willing to pay to play. But there was no way this guy could know that Scooter was a stand up kind of guy... Now.

"He invests money in your company, it ties it up, he doesn't have to pay taxes on that money. You make him money that's fine. If you lose his money that's just as good if not better because the loss won't be as much as he will save in taxes."

"I stick it to the feds any time I can," Scooter said. "What I don't like—ever—is to stick it to the common man. I'll put a bunch of money in your hand, but first I want to get a tour of the place. See the workers on the floor, that sort of thing. I leave the red tape and crap up to my team. But for my own peace of mind I need to know that I'm not dealing with people who shaft their employees. And I have a few questions about the product itself."

"What would you like to know?" Johnson asked. As he answered he stiffened, so alien or human, it was clear he knew exactly what was in the Weirdough.

"Well, for starters what is it about this stuff that makes kids like it so much? My grandson is crazy for the shit but I don't see what makes it any different from clay and putty and all that other crap that's been around forever. I sell pot, man. I don't think people buy our brownies for the taste. I need to know why kids are crazy about Weirdough, you know, if you're sticking something in it."

Aggy wanted to kick Scooter again and the question certainly didn't do anything to put Ted Johnson at ease, but he made an attempt at a laugh.

"Research has shown that the children enjoy its versatility. You can smash it and cut it...."

"Yeah, yeah I've seen the commercials. But you can't tell me it's just because you can't break it or tear it up."

"Well... it glows," Johnson said quickly.

"That it does and the truth is my grandson could tear up a crowbar in a sand box, so the fact he's still able to play with his Weirdough is a pleasant surprise. But surely there is more."

"Market research says that kids enjoy its size. Similar compounds come in small amounts; our product is the size of a softball."

"Come on. 'It's bigger.' I'm not buying that," Scooter said.

"It glows and market research shows that children enjoy things that glow."

So, "market research shows" was the guy's go to—a nice way of answering a question yet not answering it at all.

"What makes it do that? You ship it in from Chernobyl or someplace? Put a thousand mashed up lightning bug butts in each container? I can't get on board with something like that."

"I assure you, Mister Stewart the compound is completely safe. There are no toxic chemicals involved in our product or it's processing whatsoever. Not even any environmental hazards in its making. We run a clean ship." Johnson then quickly changed the subject. "In truth I think it's our interactive commercials that have made the product so popular."

Aggy pretended to be making notes but the truth was so far he had yet to tell them anything they didn't know already. *Except that they have plans to go global.*

"Yeah about that." Scooter made a face. "Kids love that guy but if you ask me Pork Chop the clown? He's kind of ... well... creepy."

"You said it, Scooter, the kids love him. I realize I refer to market research a lot, but you just can't argue with numbers. I understand many adults have a fear of clowns but we tested Pork Chop on the market beforehand and the greatest number of children responded positively to the Weirdough clown Pork Chop. The interactive commercials having the kids do things with the Weirdough at the clown's request, that's what's driving sales. We are marketing to the children, not their parents." Johnson smiled then. "In that way our business is very different from yours."

"I suppose it is but the adults have all the money," Scooter said with a grin of his own.

"Exactly and if a kid goes screaming, begging or even crying for a parent or grandparent to buy them the coolest, most awesome toy ever made, that all of his friends have and he'll simply die unless he has one of his very own, how long do you suppose the average person can hold out? And it's about product placement. Weirdough is small and so it winds up on the end caps closest to the registers. It's inexpensive so it's an impulse buy. You can't check out of any toy or department store without passing it. The kids see it, they've seen it on TV, Mom and Dad buy it for the kid or the kid has a screaming fit at the check-out line."

"Hmm, I see your point."

Aggy did, too. Corporate America sucked ass.

"Parents tune out when a commercial geared towards kids comes on and they surely do when there is a clown in it. But kids, they want to be part of what all their friends are doing."

"That's a little shady don't ya think?"

"Not at all, Scooter. No offense, but your fortune has been built on something that many people think is harmful—even evil, but you know that's not true. Even the poorest family can afford a container of Weirdough. The kids get to watch the clown interact with it and their Weirdough—everyone's happy. It's the American Dream. Create a need, supply the demand.

Kids are happy and that makes their parents happy. There is nothing at all wrong with that, it's capitalism the foundation of our great nation."

Yes except he's skipping the part where the minute the kid leaves the crap out of its box it evicts them from their body and takes it over. This guy knows exactly what's going on, I'm sure of it. If he's an alien that's bad enough but I'm pretty sure he's one of the humans helping them and that's worse. Aggy concentrated on pretending to be taking notes on her tablet.

"Why the name Pork Chop?" asked Scooter. He smiled. "Though I have to say I can see how that could play right into one of my other business investments 'cause sometimes if you're wasted ain't nothing better than a pork chop, and I bought me a slaughter house about six months ago. You think about it, it sort of ties everything together."

Which Aggy was sure it did somewhere in Scooter's mind.

Without answering Scooter's initial question Mister Johnson, looking more than a little confused, stood up. "Come with me and I'll take you on a tour of the factory floor."

The factory floor looked exactly as David had described it. But the stuff they were packaging by the thousands a minute didn't glow. Aggy knew what that meant. This factory made the product to house the soul then it went somewhere else and the soul was packed in it. She whispered in Scooter's ear not to ask why it didn't glow yet, and Scooter nodded that he understood. He did a good job of playing his part; she only hoped she was doing as well. Scooter asked floor workers how they liked their job. No one complained and all seemed generally happy to work there. Of course with the economy what it was most people were happy to just be working.

Mister Johnson was walking them out of the building after their tour and as they were walking past his office the door flew open and out walked the nightmare clown in full dress.

"There you are! Listen here, Johnson," Pork Chop bellowed in a deep voice, loud and angry as a mad bull with his sack in a vice. "Now dammit all! I thought we'd settled all this!"

He was big as life and twice as ugly as he pushed his way in front of them, successfully blocking their way out of the building.

"Now Sam, calm down, we have visitors," Johnson said looking at Scooter with meaning.

"I don't care if Jesus Christ is here, Johnson! I won't compromise my artistic integrity!"

The sweat was gathering on Aggy's upper lip and she had walked backwards till her back was against the wall, her breathing coming in quick gasps. Her hands were shaking and she quickly turned her tablet off and put it in her purse before she dropped it. Aggy took a deep cleansing breath let it out and tried to calm herself. *Dammit I didn't know I was afraid of clowns. What kind of scientist am I?*

Pork Chop was every bit as large and creepy as he'd appeared on TV. The whites of his eyes were rheumy and yellowed, sign of a long-term illness or a lifetime habit of smoking, drinking, a bad diet or all three. Big veins stood out on the backs of his hands and he looked like he should be chasing teenagers with a chainsaw in a horror movie instead of being spokesmodel for a child's toy. His makeup looked like he'd been sitting under hot stage lights for a very long time. *Sure, that'd make anybody cranky.*

"I'll be with you in a moment, Sam," said Johnson. "Just let me show our guests out. I'll come down to the studio and we can discuss these issues, sort things out. How about you head on down to the break room and have some coffee and a doughnut, sit a spell. Put your feet up. I'll be down shortly."

"Don't try to give me the bum's rush, Johnson. I created Pork Chop! I own this makeup and this look. I need to have some creative input on what I say. I *am* Pork Chop dammit!"

"Technically Sam you sold us the rights to Pork Chop when you signed your exclusive lucrative contract with us...."

"You thieving, conniving bastard..."

"Calm down, Sam." Johnson looked from Scooter to Aggy with meaning. "You are obviously scaring Ms. Jones. I know they have overworked you today, but you have all day tomorrow off, and I'm sure we can find some way to come together on this. Please let me show our guests out and then, I swear I'll be right down there and we can talk about fixing the script so that it is more agreeable to you."

"Don't blow smoke up my ass, Johnson..."

"I wouldn't dream of it." He turned from the clown and bellowed. "Janet!"

She seemed to appear out of thin air. "Yes Mister Johnson?"

"Janet, would you make sure Sam gets to the breakroom and get him something to eat and drink please?"

The pissed-off clown glared at Johnson but followed Janet away and Aggy started to breath normally again.

"Got to keep our star happy," Johnson said with a nervous laugh.

"Well I sure as hell wouldn't want to piss him off," Scooter answered.

"I hope you won't let his behavior stop you from investing with us, Scooter. You know how show biz people can be. I'm afraid the success he has had since joining us has gone right to his head. He wants more creative control; he wants more money, a bigger dressing room. He's very demanding. I'm sure you understand."

"Dude, I took drama in college so I am well aware of the tirades of actors. Aggy and I will run this by the board of directors and get back with you ASAP." Scooter shook the guy's hand. "Melodramatic screaming clowns aside it looks like you run a pretty tight ship. I'll have my guys call your guys when we've made a decision."

Johnson walked them the rest of the way to the door and opened it for them. "I hope we can do business together."

"I'm sold, but we'll have to see what the number crunchers think," Scooter said.

As they made their way to the car Aggy tried to calm herself and slow her heart down. She felt like a grade A, number one moron. *I can't believe I'm this shaky over a fucking clown! A clown! I'm glad I wore flats. I don't think I'd have made it out of the building if I'd had to walk in heels. I wouldn't mind if I could convince myself I'm this nervous because of what we were actually doing, but no this is all about the scary clown. Pathetic!* Pathetic or not she nearly ran to the van then willed Scooter to hurry up as she slammed the door shut.

Scooter got in and managed to start the van at the same time as he closed the door, which told Aggy he was not nearly as cool as he had appeared.

"Drive normal," Aggy said. "At least until we get out of the parking lot. David, you stay down."

"I know, I'm not stupid." The muffled reply came from a blanket on the back floorboards.

"And this isn't my first rodeo." Scooter was driving much slower than Aggy thought was necessary.

"You can go faster than this."

"I'm looking for the car," Scooter said.

"What car?"

"The kind of car that a very pissed-off clown would drive. You know a clown that was throwing himself a living fit because his artistic vision wasn't being realized. A clown that might accept a bribe in exchange for a little information."

"You're fucking nuts. I'm not getting anywhere near that thing again," Aggy said before she could stop herself.

Scooter looked at her and grinned. "I'm sure he doesn't wear his scary clown makeup all the time." Scooter pointed at a small yellow Smart Car. "That's it."

Aggy snorted. "Based on what?"

"A, it's bright yellow, a clown's color. B, it's environmentally friendly and that works for a dude yelling about artistic integrity. C, the bumper sticker that says I heart clowns; and D, the sign that says Pork Chop parking only."

"You could have just led with that."

Scooter shrugged speed up and drove out of the parking lot.

When they were at least a mile down the road Aggy turned in her seat reached back and slapped David on what was obviously his ass, "Wakey, wakey, eggs and bakey!"

David tossed off the blanket and scrambled up into the seat, rubbing his back. "You know I wasn't asleep, asshole. I was burning up and a nervous wreck wondering just what the hell I was going to do if you guys got into trouble. Here take this thing." He handed her the gun back and she took it and felt safe again. "Every time I heard a noise I thought I'd piss myself."

"That's okay," Aggy mumbled. "I nearly pissed myself, too."

"What?" David asked.

"Huge, angry scary clown," Scooter said. "A big, angry, scary clown. Come to think of it, I could really use a bathroom. Back to the hotel?"

"Yes please," Aggy said. The clown hadn't touched her, yet she felt like she needed to wash him off her anyway.

CHAPTER TWELVE

You Put It Where?

David had already showered and was making himself a drink when Aggy came in wearing one of the hotel robes.

"I hate to say it but creepy clowns and alien invasion aside I'm enjoying the hell out of living the high life," she said.

David nodded. He had gotten used to swank hotels—not at this level but close. At what point had he given himself over to making money instead of making a difference? He cut a covert look at Aggy where she had flopped into a recliner and was looking at her tablet and knew the answer. *When I lost her. When I gave up trying to make it work with the only woman I have ever really loved I didn't care about doing anything worthwhile anymore. I just wanted to have a bunch of nice stuff as if that could somehow replace what I'd lost—what we had and lost—and that I've never found with anyone else and if she had she wouldn't be alone now.*

"So," David started with a smile. "Did you learn anything we didn't already know?"

"You mean besides the fact that I am apparently scared shitless of clowns?"

"Yes besides that." David grinned.

"Well I think Scooter's right. I think Pork Chop would probably flip on them in a heartbeat. I'm not only sure he isn't one of the aliens but I'm sure he has no idea the product he hawks contains an alien presence."

"Soul!" The parrot squawked from the other room.

"I thought that fucking thing had gotten stoned and passed out," David said in a whisper.

Aggy just shrugged and went on. "He's the key to selling the crap, really their whole strategy. They need him but believe it or not he's a moody artist type. The other thing we learned... and this is huge... You were right. They don't put the soul in at your old plant. Nowhere in your plant because we went from the floor right to packing and to the loading dock and when they dropped a case of the crap and it broke open.... No glowing action at all. So they definitely load the alien into it someplace else."

Scooter walked in from the room he was sharing with the bird, towel drying his beard and wearing another towel tied around his waist. "I figure we try to hack their system find out where the trucks go when they leave the plant." Scooter finished towel drying his beard and threw the towel on the bar.

"So what do we do first? Try to hack their system or talk to the clown?" David asked.

"Good question. I mean the clown was pretty mad. We might want to strike while the giant iron is hot," Scooter said.

Aggy sighed. "I hate to say you have a point..."

"I got his license plate number." Scooter pointed to his head.

"Yes, like a steel trap, why don't you write it down before you forget it? I must have been more rattled than I thought I was. It didn't even occur to me to take a picture of the tag," Aggy said.

David probably would have mocked her fear of clowns except he had never really liked the damn things himself. If he had been in her shoes in the bowels of Weirdough, Inc. spying on them, and a huge screaming clown ran up on him he probably would have lost his shit, too.

"Give me the plate number so I can write it down, you know if you actually remember it," Aggy sounded pretty skeptical.

"Oh ye of little faith. I remember it," Scooter said. "It's 'I-CLOWN.' One of my exes works at the DMV. I'll see if she can get us a home address on the guy."

"If we get his address we can talk to him tomorrow. Seriously, I'm wiped completely out for today." Aggy grimaced. "The last thing I want to do to finish up the day is try to interrogate a huge, creepy-ass clown on his home turf."

"I'm with you there, Aggy," Scooter said. "I'll go check on Doobie and text my ex and give her the license plate number." Scooter went back to his room.

Aggy was engrossed in whatever she had on her tablet.

Bored, David grabbed the remote. "Aggy, do you care if I watch some TV?"

"Not at all. Find something entertaining and I'll probably watch it with you. I'm mostly going over what little I wrote down while I was in there, looking at a few of the pictures I took and trying to find something that is more helpful than the nothing I feel like we actually learned. It was a huge risk, and I would like to think there was more reward than having the clown's license plate number and knowing that he's unhappy."

David nodded in agreement and when he finally figured out how the damn remote worked started flipping through the ninety bazillion different channels. He wound up stopping on an old movie he knew almost by heart—*Dead Ringer*—because he knew Aggy loved Betty Davis. She almost immediately put the tablet down and started watching.

"There are huge, gaping plot holes you could throw a wet cat through in this movie, but she is still so good in it," Aggy said.

David nodded silently. The movie was half over when they started watching it but since they'd already seen it so many times, it didn't matter. Just like they had done over twenty years ago when they watched it together the first time they were both yelling at the character about what to do to get away with the murder.

At one point Scooter came walking in dressed in clean cargo shorts and a red T shirt. He looked from one to the other and said, "You do realize you are rooting for a murderer?"

"Her sister was a murderer, too, and a flaming bitch. She deserved to die," Aggy said.

David nodded his head as if that was a sane conclusion to come to.

"You two have some serious anger issues you need to see to." Scooter laughed. "My ex said she didn't think it would take her long then she made me promise I'd go visit my daughter and grandkids…"

"You have kids here?" David asked.

"He's got kids nearly everywhere," Aggy laughed.

Scooter shrugged at Aggy's comment which meant he didn't have a good argument for what she'd said and answered, "They're in KC actually but it's only about twenty minutes from here. My ex-wife informed me that I'd be a total flaming turd if I was this close and didn't go visit them. The whole 'I'm only here in town trying to help you two chuckleheads stop the alien invasion of our planet' didn't work as an excuse for her. She said she'd find the clown for me if I went to visit our daughter which I guess isn't too much to ask."

He left and they continued to try to help Bette Davis get away with murdering her twin, mostly by yelling at the screen that she should do this, that or the other thing, all which they knew she wasn't going to do because... Well David had seen it a half dozen times and Aggy had probably seen it dozens. The outcome wasn't likely to change no matter how much they yelled at the TV.

When the movie was over David started channel surfing again. "If you see anything you'd like to watch..."

"You know what David? My taste hasn't changed much and what I remember is that we mostly like to watch the same crap."

David took a deep breath and let it out. That was his opening, his chance to break the ice, to get the conversation going. He kept switching channels and asked what he thought would be an ice-breaking question which it was... But it turned out not to be the way he wanted the ice broken.

"So how's your mother?"

Aggy took in a long, deep breath so loud he could hear it. When he turned to look at her he could almost see a darkness descend on her features.

"She's dead."

"I'm sorry. I didn't know."

"You didn't know a lot of things, David." Aggy ran her hands down her face. "I know you liked her because she always put on a good show for you, and I never told you any different because frankly you didn't want to know. She was always good at pretending to be nice which made everything she did that much worse—because if you can pretend to be nice it's obviously a choice when you aren't.

"David, my mother was a moronic, narcissistic bitch. She thought she knew everything and knew nothing. She caused problems and then played the victim. She neglected me until she wanted to show the world what a good mother she was and then she would take me out of moth balls, dust me off and push me into one sport or activity or another whether I was interested or not. I'd maybe get dinner if she thought about it, yet she would drag me to practices or meetings and be completely invested in whatever it was until it became clear that I wasn't going to excel at it then... She'd pull me out of it whether I was enjoying it or not and I'd get a one-hour lecture screamed at a pitch dolphins could hear about how I wasn't good at anything and I just didn't know how to apply myself.

"She was so extremely vindictive that she used me to make my father suffer. She jacked him up so much on when he could and could not see me, when and where that to this day—and even though she's dead—our relationship is strained and distant. My father relates seeing me with having that bitch making him jump through some hoop or other. You never met him because I always have to go to him. He will pay for a plane ticket for me but even the idea of coming to me makes him have a near PTSD episode. See she was always getting mad and calling him to come get me. He always would and everything would be great. We'd both get used to it and then when she wanted to play mother again she would come and take me away from him. It traumatized us both every single time which just made her happy. He had to stop caring about me as much as he did or she was going to drive him insane and once you un-love someone, even just a little, you can never be as close to them again.

"She never left one man till she had another on the line and she never had a man or a friend longer than it took them to be around long enough that she got tired of pretending to be nice or even reasonable."

"I'm sorry," David said again.

"Because she was a bitch or because till this minute you didn't know? You saw her three times, David. We lived together for years and you saw her three times and what happened every time?"

"You got in a fight with her and she left."

"Yes I got in a fight with HER! She played you like she played every other man she met. Every single time she visited she was pushing my buttons as fast and as hard as she could from the moment she walked through the door. I felt like a punching bag! You never even heard it; she was a master at the art of passive aggression. She made me look like a sniping, snapping bitch to you till you went and hid as you always did every time there was the least bit of conflict. Then she hit me up for money, as if two college students living off our scholarships and what we could make working part time in fast food had money to spare.

"You didn't know what having her there did to me because you didn't want to know. You never wanted to talk about uncomfortable things or have hard conversations. You didn't know because the minute my mother and I were actually fighting you left the room or left the apartment altogether.

"The bitch died, she died without an apology to me or anyone else. She died as she lived a self-loving, hateful bitch. She died from smoking the cigarettes she loved so much. She blew them in my face my entire childhood and refused to stop smoking them even when the doctor told her they were killing her. She died, and now I'll never get an apology from her. Here's the real problem David—no matter what a parent does to you, you still love them. More than that, you need them to love you." She got up and stomped into her room shutting the door and he heard her lock it.

David stood up and started pacing back and forth. *Well I blew that, but at least now I know exactly what happened between us. She's right; I don't like conflict, and though she never talked about her childhood I talked about mine all the time so she knew why I didn't like it. My father screamed and threw fits our whole childhood, my mother said and did nothing just put up with it. Me and my siblings went and hid till the screaming stopped. They were mostly good parents for an angry bitter man and his co-dependent, condescending wife, but the last thing I ever wanted in a relationship was to fight. So I would just walk away every time things were the least bit heated between us.*

We're in our 40's and still dealing with the crap our parents' saddled us with. David stared at the closed door. *After the attack, while Aggy was healing and even after she seemed better, Aggy was mad at the world... and what did I do? I changed the subject. Every single time she tried to talk about what had happened and how it made her feel... I just didn't want to hear about it at all. Everything pissed her off and when she would lash out I would take it personally, I'd yell at her not to yell at me, I'd tell her to calm down and then I would just leave.* David had to admit that the same thing had happened to his marriage. He didn't want conflict. His wife saw that as him not caring. In fact if he was honest that's exactly what it had been—he didn't care enough about her to fight with her about anything. But he had cared about Aggy, yet he had done the same thing to her. *I shut her out. She needed to talk about what happened to her and I just shut her down. I felt so guilty; I felt like I failed her. I didn't want to be reminded of what did happen much less what almost happened. I... I made it about me. I made it about me and even though I took care of her through her physical injuries I just couldn't be there for her emotional ones because I was too selfish and self-centered to realize it had happened to her not me. I just wanted things to go back to the way they were before, and I was too young and too stupid to know that they couldn't until I let her deal with her trauma, not mine—hers. So what now, twenty years later and an alien invasion pending?*

David walked across the room and knocked on the door.

"What!?" Aggy snapped.

"I'm sorry Aggy. Sorry for wimping out twenty years ago and not being there for you on your terms, and I'm sorry for showing up now and throwing a huge turd into the middle of your life." He was about to walk away when the door opened.

"And I'm sorry that I didn't trust you enough to just tell you what I needed. That I didn't insist you listen. Instead of being so mad at you because you didn't magically know, I should have just told you what I needed you to do."

He moved to embrace her and she hugged him back. They exchanged a real hug, not the half-assed, uncomfortable hug they had exchanged back at the lab on that first day. She pulled his head down to hers and kissed him and he kissed her back. He might have felt bad about immediately getting wood except Aggy quit kissing him, took his hand and pulled him into her room. He shut the door behind him.

She turned and grinned up at him. "You know what we're doing is pretty dangerous. We might end up dead soon," Aggy said, and started unbuttoning his shirt.

"I don't think we are in any immediate..."

She cut him a look.

David nearly smacked himself in the head. "Maybe not just us, maybe the whole world. We'd better make the most of the time we have."

Aggy gave him a wicked grin and looked at the bulge in the front of his pants. "I see you remember how to get started."

"I figured why waste any time when the fate of the free world...."

Aggy was kissing him again and he was kissing her as he untied her robe. After that they didn't do much talking.

"Wow!" David flopped back on the bed and took a couple of seconds to slow his breathing. "That was better than I remembered."

Aggy laughed. "You don't by any chance think I spent the last twenty years pining away for you. I've had a few lovers. I've learned things. So have you."

David rolled on his side and put his arm over her. He kissed her cheek.

She took his hand and wound their fingers together. Her features were unreadable.

"You okay Aggy?"

She smiled. "I'm more than okay."

"I think we need to talk..."

"Why?" Aggy whined. "Can't we just lay here, maybe get some sleep? Work at not thinking about how everything we have is now sagging and pudgy and just enjoy how good we feel right now."

David laughed. "What are you saying about my bod, Aggy?"

"What I'm saying is let's not analyze it to death. We had a good talk and better sex. I don't want to start right away wondering if we're going to pick up right where we left off; we both know that's not possible. We aren't the same people—you aren't and certainly I'm not. For once in our lives let's just let something be whatever it's going to be. Let's deal with this step and not worry about the next one or if there even is one. The problem with being a scientist is that we develop theories and then we are always doing experiments to prove them. Sometimes, most times, a theory just doesn't pan out. If we have a theory about what happened before or what will happen now, then we are going to try to be right. A lot of times trying to be right ruins everything."

So it turned out that when he wanted to talk she didn't. But, as she proved when she was able to coax a second erection out of him, talking was really over rated.

CHAPTER THIRTEEN

The Tears of the Clown

"So... *I see you and Aggy* had that talk," Scooter said as David walked out of Aggy's room still only about half dressed.

David closed the door. Aggy was asleep and he figured she not only needed some sleep but deserved it.

"Yes and no," David said with a smile. "The 'no' was much better than the yes."

Scooter looked confused for a minute then grinned and started shaking his big, bald head.

"How did your visit with your kids go?"

"Good and bad," Scooter said. "The bad was better than the good." Now he looked really confused then nodded and said, "I mean the bad was lots worse than the good was good. I don't know if it just shows what brats my grandkids are or if they have a genetic disposition for stupidity that has to come from me, but I'll be damned if one of those kids isn't actin' just like the little dumplin' did. Bigger than shit when I asked, his mama had gotten him some of that fucking Weirdough. We looked and looked but didn't find that crap anywhere. But get this; while I was there I caught the little shit making a phone call, and I'm thinking he was calling the mother ship. If that's the case our cover may have been blown."

David was thoughtful. "Probably not. Remember Doobie thought your name was Grampy? The only knowledge they have about being human is what was stored in the kid's brain. The kid wouldn't have known that we went to Weirdough, Inc. today."

"I'd still like to get over there and have Aggy scare the fucking alien out of my grandkid and back into some Weirdough."

"I can make some with only a few items, and...." David did smack himself in the head then. "Dammit, given the composition of the Weirdough you could pass an electric current through it. That's why it is the perfect medium for the alien presence as long as it doesn't dry out, it allows the presence to stay without floating away. We didn't get in and play with the shit, we cut it and zapped it and a billion other things, but we didn't play with it the way a kid would."

David went to his room and came back with one of the unopened boxes of Weirdough. He opened it and started kneading it in his hands, and in a few minutes he knew exactly what the allure of Weirdough was.

"Kids like this shit because it has a slight tingling sensation. You can feel the energy of the presence and... It's imprinting on the kid a little bit all the time so that by the time it takes over the kid it's easy. That's what the fucking bird meant!"

Scooter held out his hand and David handed him the Weirdough. He kneaded it for only a few seconds than dropped it like it was hot and started jumping up and down on it. "You evil fucking shit!"

David let him have his moment and went to wake Aggy up.

When David met Deidra, Scooter's daughter with his third wife Trish of the DMV, she looked nothing like him. Yet unlike Alex—who resembled Scooter but acted like he was the spawn of Yuppies—Deidra actually looked like she should be Scooter's kid.

Deidra was living in a modest wood-frame house on the outskirts of the city. To get to the front door they had to walk down a stone path through the middle of an herb garden. The house was painted orange with black trim and from the street it looked just like a happy little jack-o-lantern. When Dedra's partner Jack opened the door he reeked of weed and he was wearing torn jeans and nothing else. Deidra came running into the room, her wild hair standing in every direction on her head, her dress floating around her in a swirl of multicolored cotton.

"Am I glad to see you."

She quickly hugged her dad then unceremoniously grabbed David's hand and started leading him down a hall way.

Aggy and Scooter followed.

"He got worse."

"I told you, Mom," a girl of about six said as she brought up the rear. "I told you he was bad."

"He went nuts when you left, Dad," Jack said, pushing the little girl back still further. "I heard him talking to someone. I found him in his closet. He was talking to someone on the phone so I took it away and stuck it on top of the fridge where he couldn't get it."

"And that's when he lost it," Dedra said. "Like something out of *The Exorcist.*"

Which seemed appropriate because when they opened the door they saw the boy's parents had tied the boy, one limb to each post of his bed, and he was screaming incoherent words and flailing around trying to get loose.

He looked right at Scooter and yelled, "Let me go bald one, or I cut you!"

"I'd like to see you try, you evil little bastard," Scooter said. But it was obvious looking at him that Scooter was pretty creeped out as he yelled. "Who are you kidding you asshole? You couldn't even reach the phone, Stubby."

"If you will just leave me alone with the boy I will administer the antidote," Aggy said, opening her bag and looking all doctor-like in her lab coat.

David really didn't want to leave the room because he knew exactly what Aggy was going to do to get the alien out of the child, and he wasn't at all sure what Aggy would do if the alien wouldn't leave the child's body. David tried not to think about it as he ushered them all out of the room because after all he couldn't think of a better way to do what had to be done.

"Can I see that phone?" David asked. He followed Jack into the kitchen.

Jack reached on top of the fridge and fished around till he found it. He wasn't a very tall guy, but still taller than the child host of an alien presence. He handed the phone to David.

"What's really wrong with our kid? And don't tell me that he ate his silly putty. I ain't buying that shit," Jack said.

"Well...." David tried to come up with something to tell him as he checked the phone log. Not too surprisingly the kid had called Weirdough, Inc., but he had been smart enough to call not text so David couldn't know what the kid might have told them. Most likely the thing had described Scooter and since Scooter was a pretty unique-looking character, they were no doubt putting two and two together.

Jack was looking at David expectantly.

David sighed. "There is an alien in the Weirdough. When you don't put it away properly it starts to die, so it takes over the kid."

Jack laughed. "Yeah, sure!"

David just shrugged and handed the man his phone back. "Well?" Scooter asked.

David didn't have to ask what he meant because they had a big discussion about it as they were packing out of their swank hotel suite.

"I think we might have been made," David said. He hated to admit it because he had been sure that Aggy was overreacting when she insisted they pack up and get out of the hotel ASAP.

"Just what the hell is going on?" Deidra demanded of her father.

Before Scooter could answer, she turned on Jack like a pit bull on a burglar. "All you cared about was that he was behaving better. I told you there was something bad wrong with him. But you didn't give a shit because you didn't have to get off your lazy worthless ass and take care of him anymore. You didn't care because he went and got you whatever you asked for and you didn't have to get off your dead ass and do a God-damned thing."

David guessed then that Jack and Deidra had more problems than that their kid had been taken over by an alien.

"Get off my back, Deidra. He has always acted like an animal because God forbid that we should discipline him and stifle his fucking creativity. You work all the time so that you don't have to spend any time with the kids. You stick me with the house work and taking care of the kids 'cause you think you're too damn good to do it then all you do is nag, nag, nag!" Jack yelled back.

Scooter never did have to answer that question his daughter asked about "what the hell was going on" which was good because David was pretty sure none of them really knew, at least not more than he'd already told them that made Jack laugh and say, "Yeah, sure."

Aggy walked into the room holding the boy's hand and the boy looked at his screaming parents and yelled, "Shut the fuck up!"

David started to think that this time Aggy's bluff had failed, but then the parents stopped screaming at each other, ran and embraced their son and said together, "He's cured!"

Scooter grinned at David and said, "Yep Hayden always has been a mouthy little fucker."

"This house is clean," Aggy said, and without another word

walked out of the house leaving them to follow or be left behind.

They spent the night in a not-so-bad hotel. They got in Aggy's name and with her card. It certainly wasn't as nice as the one they had been staying in. In the morning with the clown's address in hand they rolled out. They found the clown's house easily using the GPS in Aggy's phone.

Aggy was a little surprised to see that he lived in a run-down section of town in a house not much bigger than his clown car.

But then David said, "He's only been working for Weirdough, Inc. for a few months."

So he'd made enough money to buy the car and probably pay off outstanding debts but not enough to move out of the slums.

"What now?" Scooter asked.

It was a damn good question. They were pretty sure he wasn't one of the aliens but he might be one of the assholes who knew what he was working for. They didn't think so, but guessing was never a comfortable situation for Aggy. She liked proof. Plus it turned out she hated clowns. She wondered if the man might still be dressed in his creepy clown suit wearing his even creepier clown makeup. Aggy didn't want to look like a ginormous chicken shit but she wasn't sure even armed she was going to be able to hold onto her shit long enough to interrogate the clown if he was in his gear. Plus he was a huge guy, how strong was he? He lived in a rough neighborhood, maybe he was packing heat, after all she lived in suburbia and she carried a gun. How dangerous was this really?

"I could just go knock on the door," David said. "Ask him for an autograph for my kid or some damn thing then you know... Ask him if he is actually an alien or knows that he's working for aliens and..."

"Maybe it's time we go to the cops."

Aggy and David turned to look at Scooter like he had just pulled a dead cat out of his ass.

"Who are you and what have you done with Scooter?" David laughed.

"Dude, desperate times."

"It's like the beginning of a bad joke," Aggy said. "Two bio chemists, a stoner and a talking parrot walk into the police station and say, "I know you won't believe this but... And you know why I say the beginning of a joke, Scooter? Because after that they'll lock our happy asses up in the Ha—Ha Hilton!"

"You okay, Aggy?" David asked.

"No! That clown creeps me the fuck out. If I could come up with a better way to get more info on Weirdough, Inc., I'd do nearly anything else. But I can't. What about you two chuckle heads?"

"He creeps me out, too," Scooter said.

"I meant..." Aggy sighed. "Do either of you have an idea that means we don't have to talk to the clown?"

Because of course Aggy was pretty good at computers and so was Scooter, but they had spent the better part of a day trying to hack into the Weirdough corporate computer system and failed every time.

"I've never seen a fire wall like this," Scooter had said.

"Hey dumbass," Doobie chided. "We have interstellar technology and can extract a soul and move it to another body. Building a fire wall you dumbasses can't crack is child's play."

"Do you know how to get through the fire wall bird?" Aggy had asked.

"Do I look like a geek?"

"You look like a worthless pain in the ass we don't need," David had hissed.

Aggy ran her hands down her face. "I hate to say it, but I think we have to go talk to Pork Chop."

"It's ten in the morning and he's not working today, so chances are he will not be in his makeup," Scooter reminded her.

Aggy nodded he was right of course.

"I like Pork Chop. He's funny," Doobie said from where he sat in his cage on the seat beside her.

"Why am I not surprised!" Aggy hissed.

"Great." Scooter sighed. "He just spotted us." Scooter covertly pointed at the only window in the front of the house. "No, don't both look at once or at least be sneakier about it." He sighed again. "Oh never mind. You guys couldn't sneak up on a barrel of blind toads."

"So says the guy driving the van with a giant mural of his cartoon self in the middle of a pot leaf," Aggy said. "I'm sorry if clown stalking isn't in my repertoire."

"He's now watching us, so I'm thinking we really aren't doing this right. On a bright note he isn't in his makeup and suit," David said.

"Thank God," Aggy muttered. "Well, let's go talk to the clown."

"Oh, can I go? I always wanted to meet a celebrity," Doobie said.

"You know that's not a bad idea," David said. "If we can't convince him that what we are saying is true maybe the bird can."

"Oh, goody!" Doobie exclaimed, swinging back and forth on his perch. "We should bring him a muffin. Mommy said you should never visit someone empty handed. Get the one in the corner that's scorched."

Scooter and Aggy got out of the van followed by David awkwardly wrestling the dog crate full of parrot/alien close behind. They crossed what served as the clown's tiny front yard, covered with trash and the occasional scruffy weed patch.

Aggy thought briefly of her life's work left mostly forgotten in her lab. *Till the soil, add the right fertilizer and plants would grow even here. I should be at home, teaching classes, building the next best less-polluting fertilizer in my effort to make one that does no damage. I'm too old and too smart to be running around with my ex... Well mostly ex-boyfriend and my stoner friend confronting killer clowns about aliens.*

As they neared the front door it swung open but the screen remained firmly latched. Pork Chop the Weirdo clown, sans clown suit and makeup, filled the doorway almost completely. No doubt about it; he was a big, big man.

"Whaddya want?" rasped the big man's voice. "I already got religion, I'm diabetic so I can't eat cookies, and I ain't in the market for a vacuum cleaner or new siding. Not that it would help this dump, anyway." He coughed, a long, jagged, hacking, phlegmy-sounding rasp, and then smiled a sickly smile in their direction.

Yep no doubt about it now, he was a long-time smoker at the very least. She swallowed hard then asked, "Are you Pork Chop the clown?"

"I didn't do nothin' so don't even try to serve me papers."

"No, no sir. Nothing like that." Aggy elbowed Scooter forward, thinking Pork Chop might recognize him.

To his credit, Scooter rose to the occasion. "Mister Pork Chop—"

"Just Pork Chop, or Sam, my name is Sam."

"Sam then. I don't know if you remember me and my associate. We were at Weirdough, Inc. taking a look around the factory and all. I'm thinking of investing some serious money in the company."

He nodded his big head so quickly he looked like a bobble headed doll for a second. "Sure I do. What can I do for you?"

"I could tell you weren't happy. Between you and me I like to know that the companies I invest in are aboveboard..."

Pork Chop smiled and looked over at the van in his driveway. "Ain't you the pot king?"

Scooter laughed. "All the more reason to make sure I don't invest in anything that might get some bad press down the road. Can you tell me what you were really so pissed off about?"

"Those corporate douche bags want me to spout absolutely the stupidest crap. They pay me just enough that I don't dare walk away and they have me stuck in a contract so tight a fart couldn't squeeze out. The newest bunch of commercials they want me to do are the worst ones yet." He drew himself up, if possible, to an even larger height in the doorway. "I gotta stand up for my artistic integrity, y'know. Like it or not this is all I have and... well it looks like I don't really even have that."

"That's kind of what I thought was going on. That just doesn't seem right to me, them glomming on to your intellectual property like that. I have a team of lawyers; we might be able to get you out of your contract. Maybe you could work for us on our new ad campaign. There is no reason at all that hyperactive kids can't be sucking on pot lollies all day."

Aggy grinned and remembered that Scooter was at his core still a con man.

"You have some great appeal."

"You know what... this ain't the best neighborhood. Come on in." Pork Chop unlatched the screen door and held it open, waving them in with one hand.

They entered the small, cluttered living room. Pork Chop swept some papers and food wrappers off the sofa so they could sit down.

"Sorry for the mess. I gave the maid the day off." He laughed.

They sat down but Pork Chop didn't, which didn't put

Aggy at ease as she looked up at him.

Aggy grimaced when she saw the Pork Chop costume lying limply over the back of a battered recliner. *Looks like someone killed a clown and left the skin out to dry. I wonder if that's how he actually got it? Who's his decorator, John Wayne Gacy?*

Pork Chop looked at Scooter first, then Aggy and finally David. When he saw the dog crate he frowned. "What's that? Some yappy little dog?" The fact he couldn't see for himself told Aggy he didn't have very good eye sight.

"No it's a yapping fucking bird," Aggy mumbled under her breath.

"It's a bird—a parrot to be specific." David scrambled to cover Aggy. "He's a big fan of your commercials."

"Really?" asked the clown.

"Really. He can't get enough of Pork Chop. He knows the song and everything," Scooter said.

"Okay... kind of weird, but... let's hear it."

"Well," David said. "He's kind of a jerk. He only does it when he wants to."

"Yeah, there's a reason I don't work with birds. Tried it once and that was one time too many. Little flying shit machines." Pork Chop turned to Aggy "Sorry, ma'am."

"You didn't call her a flying shit machine," Doobie said, obviously pissed off.

Aggy began to regret their decision to bring him in with them.

The clown laughed. "Wow he is a talker. Yeah, I don't work with any animals. Dogs, monkeys, especially not ponies. Biting little shits."

"Biting little shits!" Doobie shouted from inside the crate.

Pork Chop laughed. "Hey, he sounds just like me!"

"Hey, he sounds just like me!" yelled Doobie.

"He's quite the smart ass." Pork Chop laughed.

"Better than being a huge dumb ass!" Doobie squawked. "Forget what I said about the muffin. He doesn't deserve it. He's racist against animals! He's animalist! Awk!"

Pork Chop's brow furrowed into caveman proportions as he stared at the bird, then David. "That's not funny. Are you some kind of ventriloquist? 'Cause in this case you'd be the kind that gets his whole ass kicked."

"David isn't a ventriloquist," Scooter assured Pork Chop.

"I told you the bird is a jerk," David reminded.

"Hey, you big dumb Pork Chop! Aggy is scared shitless of clowns!"

Aggy thought about reaching in the cage and choking the bird to death right there in front of God, the clown and everyone. She swallowed then said. "Nothing personal Sam." She whipped up a cover story quick. "I had a really bad birthday party when I was a kid. Clown brought nitrous instead of helium for the balloons. All the kids started tripping, Dad got drunk and bit the pony that ate my birthday cake and shit on my presents. It's nothing personal."

"And see that's why I don't work with animals." Pork Chop glared into the cage. "You're right. That bird IS a jerk!"

"Fine, I'm eating the muffin then, dick face! Yummy, that's one good muffin!" Doobie said.

"He likes them. They really aren't that good," David said. He reached for the handle of the crate and gave it a good shake.

It didn't really shut Doobie up but he was busy eating so mostly it was just the sound of Doobie chewing occasionally broken by him saying, "Yum, yum."

"Screw the bird," Scooter said. He looked confused, seemed to go over what he said trying to find what was wrong with it, gave up and then went on. "Really we don't have time to beat around the bush. We have a few questions for you, Sam."

Pork Chop glared at the crate and gave the bird the middle finger then turned his attention back to Scooter. "Alright... what do you want to know?"

"Well you seemed pretty upset. Just what exactly happened?" Aggy asked.

"I'd been in makeup and on the set for hours shooting the next set of commercials. Then I get a note from upstairs scrapping the whole day's shoot. They said they didn't like the current set of commercials and that they'd have to skip ahead to the final commercial sequence. Then I got the copy for that and it was pure crap. Worse than any of the other crap they've had me do to date. There was no flow and it just doesn't make any sense," Pork Chop finally walked over to sit on top of his costume on the recliner, thus explaining why it looked like it had been wadded up and sat on. Aggy was just glad she couldn't see it anymore.

"The final commercial sequence?" Aggy asked, her interest

piqued.

Pork Chop continued "Yeah. The commercials have been shot in sequence. As their spokesman all I did in the first few commercials was introduce the product, tell parents where to get it and sing the song. They sent me around the country putting in personal appearances at toy stores showing the kids all the things they could do with Weirdough. Then the commercials started to be more interactive." He made air quotes. "They should do what I was doing with the Weirdough, making animals, picking up news print, chopping it in two and watching it come back together. And always—always— the message about putting Weirdough away in its original container when kids were finished playing with it. I complained about the copy. I wanted to have more input. I think it's stupid to keep teaching the kids the same damn lesson—you know put your things away—I wanted to end with something like *Don't talk to strangers*, or *Eat your vegetables*."

"That sounds like a good idea," Scooter said.

"Yeah that's what I thought, so I just did it and you would have thought I shot baby Jesus with a twelve gauge. They dressed me down, told me to read only what was on the teleprompter and not to improvise at all and then... Well then they told me that we were going to shoot all the commercials coming up to their big Christmas day surprise yesterday. That's a long time in make-up and a long time under the lights in that stupid costume and the new commercials are even more stupid than the old ones. I was pissed as hell."

"Do you get paid by the commercial?" David asked.

"Yes and by the appearance. I'll tell you this they aren't paying me enough to put up with their crap."

"Have you filmed all the commercials then?" David asked.

"All but the last one. I'm supposed to do that one tomorrow. I have to tell you it's the stupidest one yet."

"And that's the one that airs on Christmas day?" Aggy asked.

"Yes."

"And why is it the worst one?" Aggy was almost afraid of the answer. Christmas was looming on the horizon only a few weeks away now. No doubt parents were buying Weirdough by the carts full. It was inexpensive and kids loved it. "What exactly was wrong with the script?"

"In every single one of the other ads I tell the kids to put the crap back in its container, but in this one I tell them to dump it out and leave it out..."

"Caaarp," David muttered.

Aggy nodded; it all made sense now. It's why they were so upset that some kids were being taken over early. The plan was to have them all taken over at once. These early possessions were a problem. It had drawn their attention; maybe it had drawn other people's as well. It's why the clown kept telling them to put it away and when to watch for the next commercial. Every kid would be glued to their TV waiting for the next installment and it would be a massive take over.

"That sucks," David said looking right at her.

"Yeah, that's what I said." Pork Chop sighed. "If there is a way to get me out of my contract... you know after they pay me for all this work."

"Did you ever handle the Weirdough? Touch it?" David asked.

"Don't you know? I thought you were a fan," Pork Chop scowled.

"I said the bird was a fan," David said. "Now, did you touch it?"

"Sure. Lots of times. I did all kinds of things to it in the commercials."

"But did you *touch* it?"

"Of course. It's kind of tingly." Then he looked at them all in turn except the bird, and it was clear he was beginning to think maybe they weren't there to give him a new job. "Is there something wrong with the stuff? I heard them talking... It's not safe is it? Well, you can't sue me. I was only the spokesclown!"

"No one wants to sue you," Aggy said. "Do you know what you're selling, Sam? Do you have a clue?" She was way tired of wasting time. Clearly they were only weeks away from a massive alien take over. She was more than ready to get some real answers if he had any.

"It's glowy, tingly goop," Pork Chop said. "What's going on here?"

"What you are selling to children all over America—and soon to go global—is an alien presence in a can," Aggy announced. She stood up and started pacing. "That's why it has to stay in the can till you have them all dump them out at once. The alien takes over the child, and then they will take over our world."

Pork Chop stared. "The kids or the aliens?"

"The aliens in the kids," Scooter explained.

"But... how? They're just kids."

"They won't stay kids, and some of them aren't kids now. You have been working with some of them; you didn't know any difference, did you?" Aggy asked.

"Oh," Pork Chop started to laugh. "I'm being punked..."

Aggy stopped pacing and stared down at Pork Chop. "That bird is such a jerk because he's not a bird at all; he's one of them that we stuck in a parrot's body. Have you ever in your life heard of a bird that can talk like that one? You aren't stupid. Think about it, you said it yourself the ads don't make any sense."

"Am I on *Candid Camera*?" Pork Chop asked suspiciously.

Aggy sighed. "It's a long story." She sat down hard next to David on the couch and looked expectantly at Doobie.

"You tell him."

Pork Chop sat and absorbed what the alien—possessed parrot told him.

When Doobie had finished Aggy looked at Pork Chop. "I know that's a lot to absorb, and I know how crazy it must sound especially coming from a bird."

"Hey!" Doobie objected.

"What do you need from me?" Pork Chop asked.

"You believe us then?" David asked.

Pork Chop nodded. "I believe the bird. Like you said, I ain't stupid. I may not have the kind of education you folks have, but even I know ain't no regular parrot can talk like that. Also, those people at Weirdough, Inc.—they don't act right and they wouldn't if they were what you say they are. So again I ask... What do you need from me? Look, I'll be the first to tell you that I ain't the greatest guy in the world. I've made a lot of mistakes in my life, but I haven't—and wouldn't—do anything to hurt a little kid. You don't become a clown unless you like kids. Clowning... it's in my blood."

Aggy got an all-too-clear picture of tiny cars and clowns running around with spritzers and big hammers through the big guy's arteries.

"No one likes to be made to look stupid. I don't like being used by these fuckers, and it's not just my name they are ruining it's all of clown kind. I don't want to think about a world where kids no longer trust clowns. So what can I do?"

"If it's any consolation they used me, too. I'm the one who invented the stuff they put the alien into," David said. "The Weirdough made at this plant is safe. It doesn't glow and has no alien in it when it ships out. Somewhere between here and when it goes onto the store shelves they add the alien presence...."

"Do you mean soul?" Sam asked

David looked at Aggy and sighed. "If that's what you want to call it. Do you know where the trucks go after they leave the factory?" David asked.

Aggy nodded that was a good question and he was sort of cute when he was using his brain.

"And see right there I should have known they were up to no good." Pork Chop looked defeated. "One day I was in the break room with a couple of the drivers. We're just bull shitting and I asked where they were headed, you know just making small talk. They look at each other and then one of them tells me that they aren't allowed to say where they go and if they do they automatically get fired. I feel so stupid. Why would a normal toy company have to hide where the trucks go after they leave the factory? Maybe I could find out, spy on them."

"I don't think that's a good idea...." Aggy started.

"Should I just go into work, business as usual?"

"Yes, if you can do it without drawing attention to yourself," David said.

Pork Chop nodded. "Of course I can. I am an actor after all."

Suddenly Aggy had a Eureka moment. "I know just how to foil their evil plan."

"You did not just say that," David laughed.

Aggy smiled. "Sometimes the classics are appropriate."

CHAPTER FOURTEEN

A Hemp Scout Is Kind and Courteous and Really, Really Laid Back

Pork Chop turned out to be a good recruit to their cause. He quickly put together what Aggy called the final solution and when they saw what he had produced they were all happy with it. Turned out the creepy-looking guy had some real talent.

They had tried hanging out in the truck stop near the plant, but Pork Chop was right, David had no idea what they were paying the truckers or if they were all aliens but either way none of them would tell anyone where they went when they left the plant. He said as much to Aggy who was sitting on the only chair in their hotel room.

"I'm afraid if we get too pushy they'll know we're up to something," Aggy said, "we're running out of time."

"I think we need to quit trying."

"They leave the trucks unguarded overnight sometimes before they get loaded when the plant opens. If we could stick some sort of GPS system on one of them we could follow them to the mother ship," David said.

"I just happen to have one of those," Scooter said with a grin.

They were all standing around the rear of the van getting ready for the next step of the almost plan they had.

"Where the hell did you get a tracking device?" David asked Scooter.

Aggie answered, "Come on, David, rich people can get anything. A person with connections to crime with money...."

"Harsh, Aggy. It's just GPS technology. I got it off the internet. You can get anything off the internet... You know if you have enough money." Scooter grinned.

David looked at the device in Scooter's hand and swallowed hard. He didn't want to do it, but he wouldn't—couldn't—let either of them do it. After all it was his fault they were involved at all and they had already gone into the belly of the beast once. Still he wasn't thrilled about trying to stick the magnet holding the tracking device under the bumper of one of the trucks. He took the device from Scooter and turned to look across the abandoned field. He could clearly see the lights of the factory; they were closed and locked down for the night. But because David had worked there he knew the trucks— the ones to be loaded the next day—were parked on the road just outside the factory unguarded. All he had to do was get across the field unseen and stick it on the bumper. The only real problem was these were sleeper trucks. The drivers were all in their cabs and not all of them were actually asleep. There was no security but if he tripped and made a bunch of noise—and he was pretty clumsy on good days—he might get caught. He couldn't afford to get caught... by anyone.

He was dressed in black from head to toe. He even had a black ski mask on—this was also something Scooter just happened to have with him like the tracking device. He took a deep breath decided to go back to his theater roots and pretend he was playing a ninja. He took off across the barren field at a run.

Aggy giggled and looked up at Scooter. "So all that ducking low and zig zagging—you suppose he thinks that makes him less conspicuous?"

"Does the rolling help?" Scooter chuckled.

"You know he's going to wind up with a cockle burr in his butt."

"Probably." Scooter looked down at her through slanted eyes. "So... Did you makeup or did you just have sex because he was handy?"

Aggy sighed and looked at where David was making his way across the field. She hoped no one was looking because what he was doing would draw more attention to him, not less.

"I don't know. I think so. You know I thought I was completely over him till I saw him again. You and I both know that he and I don't know each other anymore. We are both very different people but... well I think I like the person he is now better than the man I knew before. Don't push it, Scooter. Let's just see what it wants to be this time, alright?"

Scooter nodded. "It's just sort of nice to have both my

friends back and you know in the same place at one time."

Aggy popped him in the ribs with her elbow. "I know, but don't be such a yenta."

Much to her dismay Scooter launched into his rendition of "Matchmaker, Matchmaker" complete with the dance moves... Yeah, if they didn't get caught it was going to be a miracle, of course when she thought of it Scooter was a diversion from what David was doing.

"We had such a nice hotel room. Then we had a not-as-nice one, and now this one sucks," Doobie said from where Scooter had set him on the dresser.

For once David had to agree with the bird. David knew the trucks normally loaded and left by eight AM, so they had found a motel close to the factory which... well when he thought of it "suck" was a nice word for the hole they were staying in.

In her bag of tricks Aggy had an organic bed bug spray she was working on in the lab and she had sprayed the entire room before she would even let Scooter take the bird much less their luggage in.

There were two beds—both equally uncomfortable. The best thing you could say about the place is that the thread—thin sheets looked like they had been washed since they were last used. The shower and toilet were hard—water stained but mostly clean, so David took a hot shower. When he walked out in his pajama pants towel drying his hair he looked at where Aggy was sitting on the bed with a pizza box in her lap a slice in one hand as she tried to switch channels with the other.

When she saw him looking she said, "Just honing up on my multitasking skills."

"So glad to see that you have been reunited with your one true love." He grinned then frowned. "I've got a sticker in my back." David had tried to rub it out by buffing his back with the towel.

Aggy put her slice of pizza in the box and set the channel selector down. She walked over to him, still chewing, took the towel from him and moved him into better light. She grumbled incoherently then went to the end table to get her glasses. When she returned she started digging in his back with her nails, and he winced.

"Isn't that a little unsanitary and... ouch!" David yelped.

"Please! Pizza sauce kills all bacteria. Everyone knows that. Got it," Aggy said, and showed him the splinter on her finger nail.

"Thanks Aggy," David said. He turned around to look at her she smiled and kissed his cheek.

"Scooter you mind if I use the shower next?" Aggy asked.

"Not at all." Scooter flopped on the other bed and stretched out. He was on his phone texting before she could gather her clothes together. She shut the door to the bathroom and David stared at it.

It was just a kiss on the cheek and after what they'd already done he shouldn't have been so excited by it. Except... well sometimes sex happened and didn't really mean anything but the little peck on the cheek she had just given him seemed intimate.

"If you two have sex again can I watch?" Doobie asked, swinging on his perch. "I would like to observe the human coupling ritual visually. I heard you doing it and it was rather ugly sounding, sort of squishy and slappy and wet in an all wrong ways. And all the groaning... Why when I first heard you I thought you were slaughtering an animal. Then I thought you were praying..."

"Shut up you wretched thing!" David ordered as Scooter cracked up. "You, too," David said to Scooter.

"Alright," Doobie said. "But can I watch? I'm very interested..."

"No you can't watch," David said.

"So... you don't even want to try to be my friend."

"Not really, no and... Humans don't watch each other have sex," David said.

Scooter had not listened to him when he asked him to stop laughing. "Whatever dude, there is a bazillion-dollar empire resting on the whole 'people watching people screw' thing," Scooter said, still just texting away.

"So why can't I watch you and the female?" Doobie asked.

"Well you are a creepy alien that took over a little boy for one thing," David said.

"Wow you people really do hold a grudge," Doobie whined. "Just because I took over some kid you won't let me watch you and your female mate."

"Dude, they are way too uptight for that. I'm their friend and they never let me watch. If you'll lay off David for a minute

I'll get you some porn up on the lap top," Scooter said.

"Don't cater to the creepy thing." David found a mostly clean t shirt in his suitcase and put it on. Scooter was still laughing. "Seriously, dude stop. You are just encouraging it. Who are you so rapidly texting?"

"My women and kids. We all try to get together in Denver for Christmas. I need to hurry and save the world and get back to send this one and that one tickets and then be there on time or my life won't be worth living."

Scooter put his phone down got up walked over opened the pizza box and took out a slice. Then he held the box out to David.

David sighed and took a piece. When he had gone in to take a shower Aggy had asked Chinese take-out or pizza? Apparently Scooter had voted for pizza and David had been voted down, or Aggy just ordered pizza because that was what she wanted. He smiled.

"So," Scooter said. "When she gives you a little, the irritating things she does become cute?"

"Well of course," David said with a shrug and ate his pizza.

At seven-thirty in the morning the tracking device went off. They had apparently changed their loadout times since David had worked there.

"This close to Christmas they have probably doubled up on production," Aggy said, forcing herself to her feet.

"They had the equipment and the staff to do that. Shit," David said, rubbing his hands down his face in an attempt to become more fully awake.

Since they had barely woken up and hadn't attempted to get out of bed till the alarm on the tracker went off, the next fifteen minutes saw them falling all over themselves and each other as they packed and dressed then stuffed things into the van however they would go in.

The bird was screaming the whole time—mostly, Aggy was sure, to make damn sure they didn't forget him—which she really wanted to.

As they pulled out onto the access road, Doobie started singing. "On the road again, just can't wait to get on the road again. The life I love is making music with my friends—"

"Shut it, bird," Aggy snapped. She slung a stale Cheeto she'd just found in the floor boards into the front of his cage.

"They only thing I hate worse than you is country western music."

"Why you gottah be like that, Aggy? He's not half bad," Scooter said. "Did you know Willy Nelson is a personal friend of mine?"

"Really? How shocking!" Aggy said.

David laughed. "I hate country western music, too, but even I know that thing is no Willie Nelson."

"No, but he could sing back up for him," Scooter said, looking as if he'd just had the most brilliant idea in the history of mankind. "Willie and the Doobie! This idea has legs."

Doobie started to sing again and Aggy turned and glared at him. "I'm going to have me some little bitty bird legs for breakfast if you don't shut the fuck up." The bird started to sing any way and she pointed at him. "Dead serious, pecker head, I'm not fit to put up with humans much less you till I get some coffee in me."

Which could be hours because she would just about bet that the trucker had packed himself a steaming thermos of the black gold and was probably peeing in an empty bottle to cut down on his number of stops to make better delivery time.

"How far ahead of us can we let him get?"

"Well it's GPS, but if he gets more than seventy miles ahead of us I'm not so sure we'd be able to find where he went if he got off the beaten track too far. You know how these things are. They're just fine unless the area hasn't been mapped. Then they're kind of useless," David said from the back seat. "I think we need to stay pretty close just to be on the safe side."

"Sorry 'bout that, Aggy," Scooter said. "Let me get a little closer to him and then we'll stop and get some Joe. But we need to go right in and right out."

Aggy didn't have to ask why he said that. He was implying that no woman could possibly go in take a pee and be back in the car in less than thirty minutes, but the truth was she didn't fart around in a public restroom. When they had finally stopped on their way to KC because Scooter had to take a dump… Forty minutes later they were on the road again. She didn't say anything because anything she would have said about it at that point would have been completely bitchy. Aggy didn't pretend to know what most women did when they went to pee that took forever, but she sure as hell didn't know why it took men an hour to shit.

She sighed a "longing for caffeine" sigh. Even if there had been a coffee maker in the room they wouldn't have had time to make any. It was probably a good thing the cheap-ass hotel didn't have one. No telling what other purpose it might have been used for—maybe making meth or maybe a urinal. She supposed she should be considering doing something about her obvious coffee addiction, but all things considered that was the least of her worries.

David had watched out the window as they were leaving town. When he had lived there he had driven to work with blinders on, never really seeing anything. But as they were leaving he had looked at everything, every tree, every building, every sign as if he were seeing it for the first time, and he admitted he really was.

He had let himself become just another cog in the wheel, reporting to other cogs and higher ups that called him "Dr. Egghead" or "tech nerd". There was no actual respect for what he did or the years of school he'd paid for in time and money to do it. His life had become making it through the work day until time to go home and do the same nothing he had done the day before.

Every day was just like the one before, on and on and ever on. David did the job to make the big bucks to pay for a bunch of expensive crap that he also never looked at didn't need and rarely used. Coffee makers that made one cup of coffee and a mountain of waste. A house full of rooms he never went in filled with the thousands of things commercials told him would make his life better and show people he was a vital, successful man.

He had become a drone running the corporate machine. How long would he have continued to do that if he hadn't found out what he was really working for? He had done it so long that he never even realized how pointless his life had become, how completely devoid of real purpose. His life was empty, and he had been lonely without realizing it till he was spending time with people he loved again.

Now he was on the adventure of a lifetime and if they were successful....

Scratch that, WHEN we are successful, we will have saved a bunch of kids from being taken over, maybe even the world.

Now when I look out the window I see things, not just flashes of color as I drive by with my only goal to get to or from work. Now I realize that people live in those houses, that they have lives there. He looked briefly at Aggy. *I have a chance to have something I thought I'd lost forever and all because I didn't look away when I saw something wrong. Because I decided to make a stand I feel really alive for the first time in years. When I think of how close I came to doing and saying nothing I'm ashamed of the man I let myself become. But I'm filled with hope because now I know I have the power to change.*

He hoped they succeeded, that he, Aggy and Scooter weren't about to be made to "disappear" like characters in a spy movie. David was beginning to understand what all those gurus were talking about when they said to be present, because if he just thought about what they were doing right then and didn't dwell on the fact they might all die he was really happy. He probably would have delved deeper into his voyage of self-discovery, but it was at that moment the damn bird decided to start singing again, and off-key to boot.

"We all live in a yellow submarine, a yellow submarine a yellow..."

"Hey little green dumbass," David hissed. "Regular birds can sing. What's your problem?"

"It's not country western," Doobie pointed out.

"Dude why you got to harsh the little guy's mellow? I love that song." Scooter defended the bird.

"How high are you?" David asked.

"I'm not."

"Then there is no excuse. That bird cannot sing! Or at least he shouldn't."

"Everyone's a critic," Doobie chimed in, and then started singing again.

Aggy turned in her seat to glare at the bird. "It sounds like somebody flushed a cat down the toilet then tried to clear the clog with a chainsaw. How 'bout we play an exciting round of 'everyone shut the fuck up'."

"Bitch!" Doobie squawked.

David took hold of the cage and shook it violently.

The bird glared at David. "So it has been proven the universe is full of assholes. It's not just us."

"Now kids quit fighting or I'll pull this car right over," Scooter announced with a grin. "Everyone take a deep breath and chillaxe, looks like we're getting pretty close to the tractor trailer rig so we should be able to stop in a few minutes."

A few minutes later David saw the Weirdough, Inc. truck. On the back doors looking back at him was an ad featuring smiling—and unaware of global take over—girls and boys happily enjoying their Weirdough, with their old pal Pork Chop waving at them intoning in a word bubble, "Get your Weirdough today!"

Aggy sighed. "I still think we would be better off in something less conspicuous than this van... you know like anything else."

"Relax," assured Scooter. "We're not getting close enough to them for them to make us. This early. There's a lot of rush-hour traffic, and in case you hadn't realized it by now I'm a pretty stealthy driver. All those years dealing drugs don't ya know?"

"Yes, we've all heard your stories about the lucrative business of hiding cocaine in your bum for fun and profit." Aggy looked back at David and rolled her eyes. David smiled back.

"Well, it wasn't always fun, especially that time when the Cartel thought... y'know what? Never mind. I'd like for you guys to have plausible deniability," Scooter said. "Looks like there is an exit ahead; stopping will probably put just enough distance between them and us."

"Don't immediately forget and go past it like you did the other day," David said. He'd nearly pissed himself that day.

"I won't forget. Pot Scouts honor."

"Pot Scouts honor?" asked Aggy.

"Just a little something I'm working on. I'm thinking kids need some direction these days. They'd start out as Weed-blows, then be Cannabis Cubs and then Pot or Hemp Scouts—I really haven't decided yet. I keep waffling like a Republican in a fourteen-way debate."

"What the hell would you teach the kids, Scooter? How to roll a joint?" David asked, laughing.

"Not right away." He grinned then said, "No really dude it's like they could start out helping little old ladies across the street to get to their dispensary to buy the pot they need for their glaucoma. It just came to me one day, what do regular scouts do really? Nothing worth a shit, that's what. They teach them to be the next generation of entitled douchebags mostly. Maybe have them do some stupid-assed arts and crafts project that strips real creativity away from the kids. They might learn how to make fires and tie knots, sleep in a tent, whoopty doo! If you have real parents they'll teach you all that shit. Mostly they shove so-called 'Christian values' down kids' throats and try their damndest to make them into the kind of people who are happy to work for the corporate machine day in and day out. The type who just follow blindly along down to vote for the douchebag of the week. How does that really serve mankind? It doesn't. Think about what pot does; it mellows people out, and it cures diseases of the mind and body. A pot scout would be taught to connect to their spirit, to care for the planet, to have their own thoughts and create in their own way. Do you have any idea how much oxygen an acre of pot makes? If they each grew their own plant... well, they'd learn all about nature and stuff. They could donate their weed to the needy."

"We could work together on this, Scooter, my clean crap, your seeds could equal world peace."

Her sarcasm was wasted on Scooter. "That's a great idea! I mean I've already been testing your shit by growing my shit in it," Scooter said. "Having a doctor on board would certainly give the pot scouts some legitimacy."

Aggy ran her hands down her face then said, "I'm gonna close my eyes and when I open them again I better see a convenience store and smell coffee."

It was nearly midnight and they had been driving south all day. Aggy had no idea where they were much less where they were going, but she figured that if she rolled down the window she'd hear banjo music. This was only confirmed when she saw the "Entering Alabama sign."

Scooter had reached his limit and was asleep on the back seat and so thankfully was the bird. David was driving and they were having the kind of conversation you could only have when you were driving for hours in the dark.

"...so what would make a good club symbol?" David asked.

"A giant psychedelic picture of Jerry Garcia." Aggy chuckled. The longer they had this conversation the funnier they thought everything they said was.

"No that would have 'our Founder' written under it." David laughed.

"How about a giant joint with wings on it and the words *E Potibus Urban* on a ribbon across the bottom for their crest?"

"The song would be *One Toke over the Line*."

"The whole uniform would be made from hemp fibers..."

"It would be tie-dyed."

Aggy's hand shot up as if she was eager to answer a question in a grade school class. "Instead of badges they would pin rolling papers to their lapels saying what skills they had accomplished."

"Hemp seed curing."

"Selling the most cannabis brownies at the bake sale."

"Sitting idly for hours talking about everything you are going to do, and never doing a damn thing."

"Oh that's a good one," Aggy said, nodding. "Swearing... with conviction... to seeing things that don't exist...."

"Like a human soul," Scooter chimed in from the back seat, his voice full of sleep. "I don't know if you assholes are digging my idea or ripping on it, but either way if you don't pull over soon we're going to run out of gas."

It was the only place they'd seen for miles, so David pulled over because there wasn't really a choice. If he could have found any other place that's where he would have stopped because this place looked like something out of an old episode of *Twilight Zone*. Unfortunately the van's low fuel light had been flashing for several minutes, and as far apart as the gas stations had gotten he was afraid this might be their last chance. Besides, Aggy had been doing the dance of the unrelenting need to pee for the last thirty miles.

Aggy went running into the store and a few seconds later she ran out and ran to the laundromat next door so David guessed that was where the bathroom was.

He couldn't use his card in the pumps, they were that old. The hand-lettered sign taped on the pump said "Pay inside before pumping", so he walked inside and Scooter was looking at him with his eyes wide. David didn't have to ask why. The inside was even worse than the outside. There was an old glass-fronted pop fridge and inside there were plastic-wrapped homemade sandwiches and cans of cheap soda sitting on the same shelf as filth-covered Styrofoam cups claiming to hold night crawler fishing worms. The cash register sat on a glass case which was filled with the lost treasures of the Disco era.

It wasn't even good bling, it was just big and gaudy and looked heavy. It might double as a weapon in a gang fight. If you fell in a pool with it on you'd most likely drown. The greasy guy behind the counter said, "We don' like hippies 'round here."

"Ah, we're not hippies, we're biochemists," David said.

"Don't know what that is, but we don't like smarty-pants people neither," he said. He had about three good teeth; the rest were all rotted brown shards.

"I need forty dollars' worth of gas," David said, holding out the money.

"Whichever way you're going the next station is a good forty miles. If you need forty, it will cost ya sixty."

"What the...?"

"Is that gal with you? She's a good-lookin' gal. She your sister? I'll knock off an extra ten bucks if ya get me a date with her, if ya know what I mean." He gave David a lewd, meaningful wink.

"Now see here fuck tard..." David started.

Scooter put his hand on David's chest, and for a minute he thought he was about to get some peace and love speech. When he looked at Scooter he knew that wasn't the case.

"I got this, Dave." He looked at the man across the counter then yelled, "Fuck you, you toothless piece of shit!" He took the money out of David's hand and shoved it back in David's pocket.

"Go put the gas in the van."

When David had been sane—before he found out there were soul-sucking aliens living in the Weirdough putty he had created—he would have tried to talk Scooter down. Instead he looked at the creep across the counter and grinned.

"Man, did you fuck with the wrong hippie."

The guy moved like he was going for a gun.

"Just do it!" Scooter yelled. Then he grabbed the guy by his collar and dragged him over the counter.

David stopped at the door in case Scooter needed help.

"Go on; fill the fucker up."

David nodded and went to do as he was told. As he was gassing the van up he heard the sound of Scooter beating the living shit out of the guy. So it turned out ole Scooter hadn't changed as much as David thought. He was still an easy-going, laid-back kind of guy till you pissed him off, and then he was a serious bad ass. He figured if Scooter needed any help he'd holler.

Back in college David had feared the trouble Scooter's rampages were going to cause them... But now, well, they couldn't really get in much more trouble than they were already in. The pump clicked off and with the tank full David scrambled back into the van starting the engine even as he finished sitting all the way down, just like a getaway driver—which in this case he was.

He had just clicked his seat belt when first Aggy came running and jumped in the passenger's seat, slamming the door. Then Scooter—carrying a burlap bag full of something—jumped in the back. As he slammed the door Scooter yelled, "Go, go go!"

David already was. He stomped his foot on the accelerator and tried to keep his eyes on the road while he tore away from the old station. He kept stealing nervous glances at Aggy then at Scooter, who he could see in the rear view mirror.

"What happened back there?"

Scooter started to answer, but Aggy yelled over him. "Holy shit, you'll never believe me in a million years! That place is the worst, most horrible restroom on the entire fucking planet! I swear! The toilet and sink looked like they hadn't been cleaned since the dawn of time! There were bugs coming out of the soap dispenser—the damn soap dispenser! The floor looked like it had been covered in blood like a slaughterhouse and the mop bucket in the corner was FULL of rusty—or was it bloody—water. If I hadn't had to go so damn bad I would have held it until we went to, oh, I dunno, the seventh level of Hell! That's how bad the commode was. And that laundromat I went through to use the restroom? That must be where they clean all the clothes from their murder victims so they can re-sell them in that piss-poor excuse for a gas station. HOLY SHIT!"

"That bad..." David started, but she cut him off.

"I had to levitate over the toilet seat so I wouldn't touch it! I'll never sleep with both eyes closed again! I'll never use another public restroom unless I have an escort of armed guards! And bug spray, lots and lots of bug spray."

"Guess I won't tell you what the king of the Redneck Nation said about you then."

"What? What could he possibly have said that could be worse than that bathroom?" Aggy asked.

David cut her a look. "He sure thought you were pretty..."

"Alright stop right there. It is worse already."

"I was going to defend your honor but there was a sudden return of ole ass kicking Scooter," David said with a grin.

"Really? Do tell," Aggy said, turning in her seat to look at Scooter.

"You know I don't mind being called a hippie at all except when someone means it to be an insult, but I'm sure not going to let him get away with saying something like that about a woman, *any* woman, and certainly not my best friend. I beat the dog shit out of that jackass and stuffed his mouth full of that God-awful crap he called jewelry. Bastard ought to consider it free dentistry. I broke off most of what was left of his fucking nasty-assed teeth. I hate people like that; go out of their way to be ass hats. Taking advantage of people just because they're different... Like being just like him would be anything anyone would want to strive for. We're on a mission from God! You know what none of us need right now? Some toothless bastard making things difficult that shouldn't be. Worse than that he is the reason people make fun of Southerners and think they are all a bunch of hateful, bigoted dumbasses." Because of course Scooter had been raised in Oklahoma. "He got the whipping he deserved, or at least enough of one he'll remember it the next time he tries to screw someone over when they stop for gas."

Scooter adjusted the large bag at his feet. It sounded like BB gun pellets or metal nuts rattling in cans whenever the bag shifted or moved.

"Um, Scooter Claus, what you got in that great big sack?" David asked.

"Well I didn't steal any of that jewelry that's for damn sure. Hell that shit wouldn't even make a decent present for one of my ex-wives. They all have better taste than that... except maybe Lorraine. I didn't clean out his cash register, either, if that's what you're getting at."

"If not money, jewelry or heaven forbid homemade baloney and night crawler sandwiches, then what?" David asked.

"Spray paint. A shit-ton of spray paint. We are obviously in the very bosom of redneck country, the land of small-minded folks that hate anything different or creative. Truth is, most of these toothless bastards probably smoke the shit out of pot but they sneak around and do it and think everyone else should, too. As much as it pains me to say it, we're gonna have to paint the van. First chance you get, pull over." Scooter sniffed sadly. "I really like the paint job. It would kill the boys back at the shop if they knew."

Aggy reached back with a tissue and after Scooter took it she patted him on the knee thinking, *I will NOT say "I told you so."*

They stopped at a rest stop on the edge of the highway and by "rest stop" she meant there was a wide spot in the road with a couple of security lights and a half dozen fifty-five gallon drums for trash cans which apparently were too small for anyone to hit. The ground was covered with litter. Aggy hopped out of the van then opened the door for Scooter. She took the bag of spray paint from him as he got out. David joined them there a few seconds later.

"Let's get this over with," Scooter said as he climbed out of the back of the van. There was an air of resignation to his voice as he added, "We're all gonna have to take a can pick a spot and get to spraying if we want to keep up with the truck."

As they each grabbed a can David quickly held up his hand. "Wait! We can't leave Doobie in the van. The fumes might kill him."

"You know if you keep saying things like that," mocked Aggy, "We're going to think you like the damn thing."

David shrugged. "He's obnoxious but still occasionally helpful. He'd be less obnoxious dead but also a lost less helpful."

"Dude we have to close the door to paint the van anyway. He'll eat fewer fumes than we will. Plus I huffed quite a bit of paint in the day, and I'm okay," Scooter said. "Let's just get this done and get the hell out of here."

Aggy thought okay was relative. She worked on the back while David and Scooter each took a side. Scooter had taken every can of yellow spray paint the little store had, but it didn't come close to matching the paint color the shop had used. To his credit he'd also grabbed a couple of cans of white and Scooter explained that the darkest part of the designs— the pot leaves in the logo especially—needed to be blocked out with the white to help cover it up when it was time to spray on the yellow.

"That makes sense," David said. "How'd you know that?"

"Tagging. I used to paint on railroad box cars, bill boards, overpasses, all kinds of surfaces."

"Was that you that painted 'Everybody must get stoned' on the front wall of the student union in college?" Aggy asked.

"I can neither confirm nor deny." Scooter grinned.

"Too bad," said Aggy. "I was going to say it was a masterpiece of Rembrandt proportions."

"How about this?" David called from the other side of the van. "I'm like Van Gogh here."

Aggy and Scooter joined David on his side and stood back looking at his paint job.

"Nice strokes there, David." Scooter said.

"More like he's had a stroke. Looks like Monet to me. It's okay at a distance, but up close it's a big old running, dripping mess."

David made a face. "If the idea is to cover it then I think I've done that. It doesn't have to be perfect but it does need to be good enough not to draw any attention. Low profile. I've done what I intended to do and that makes me an accomplished artist."

"Yeah whatever, dude."

Scooter looked at Aggy. "He has a point. He covered his faster than we did. Come on Aggy, let's finish up and get back on the road."

Scooter started shaking his can of yellow spray paint and walked back to the side of the van he was painting.

"Are you idiots finished yet? I can't see a thing from in here and the fart one of you so kindly left makes it smell like a buffalo died in here. I'd have been safer if there were paint fumes. Hurry up! I'm bored and running out of air!" Doobie shouted from inside the van.

Aggy frowned. "Well he was quiet for a minute; it was a nice break while it lasted. Too bad he didn't get any brain damage from the fumes, although I may have." Something on the ground caught her eye and she looked down to see a hypodermic syringe sticking through a spent condom. "Well that's a first." She pointed it out to Scooter.

"Man if that was in there when he was wearing it... that's hard core."

David had switched sides and finished up the small part that Scooter hadn't while Scooter rummaged around in the back of the van. He came out smiling, holding a screwdriver and a set of license plates different from the ones already on the van.

"Just happened to have those lying around?" Aggy asked as she went to help him mostly by holding things while he was changing the plates out.

"A pot scout is always prepared," Scooter answered, with a smile.

Once they got back out on the highway Scooter checked the tracker and found that they hadn't lost too much time or distance with their impromptu art project side trip. The rig they were following took an exit then turned onto a two-lane road shortly after, so they knew the factory must be getting closer. Scooter, back in the driver's seat, hung back to avoid arousing the suspicion of the truck driver.

David had balanced Doobie on the front passenger seat and secured the crate with the seat belt. He claimed so that he and Aggy could sit together and make some kind of plan about what they were going to do when they got to the factory, but he could have done that if she was sitting in the front seat. He mostly just wanted to sit by her almost as much as he didn't want to sit by Doobie—which was a lot.

"Tell the truth, you two just want to relive your ill-spent youth necking like teenagers in the back of my van," Scooter said. But he turned his attention back to driving and turned on the radio.

Doobie didn't sing along, to everyone's relief, instead mumbled quietly in his crate while they drove along that unlike all of them he preferred the back seat. And why did no one care what he wanted? He was easily ignored, or maybe they were all just getting good at it.

"We probably should have made some kind of plan before now," Aggy said with a tired smile. "I mean we are assuming that this is where they are adding the alien presence but if that's the case... Well, what then?"

It was a damn good question. One that he didn't think any of them had really thought about till Scooter said with conviction, "We blow the fuckers up, that's what we do."

"What happened to 'peace and love' Scooter?" Aggy asked.

"He had two of his grandchildren possessed by aliens, had a hill ape talk shit to him, and then had to paint over the coolest paint job he'd ever had on a van," Scooter said with conviction. "It changes a man."

David didn't even ask if Scooter actually had the stuff to blow anything up. He was pretty sure he had just about anything that any of them would ever need packed into the back of that van. In fact the entire trip David had just been rejoicing the fact they didn't all blow up when the alien rear-ended them.

"I think I should go in alone," David said.

"What are you, crazy?" Aggy hissed back.

"I'm serious. Neither you or Scooter would be in any part of this if it wasn't for me...."

"Hello, numbnuts, that crap took over two of my grandkids," Scooter reminded.

David ignored Scooter. "By now they are no doubt more worried about Scooter than they are me and Scooter has about a million children and grandchildren...."

"Oh at least that many." Aggy grinned.

"I'd never be able to live with myself if something happened that took him away from his immense family. Not to mention the hundreds of thousands of people who depend on him for their pot. He's doing a lot of good, in his own Scooter way, and I don't want to mess that up either."

"Yes, I mean what would the world do without Pot Scouts? All those old, blind women weaving their way through city traffic trying to get their glaucoma medication," Aggy said.

"That's what I thought. You *were* making fun of my idea," Scooter mumbled.

Aggy smiled at David. "Look I don't have kids or grandkids. All I have is my research on clean crap, my pizza and caffeine addictions, and maybe somewhere in my filthy house a dead cat. I've accomplished next to nothing, nobody would miss me longer than it would take to fill my position at the university and find another scientist eager to use my research to jump start theirs."

"Aggy, that's not true."

"I'm not whining or fishing for compliments, David. Right this minute I can't think of anything I care about more than I do you, so what I'm saying is that if you're going in so am I. Wither you goest I shall go and all that good rot. One for all and all for one."

"I couldn't have gotten this far without you, but I don't want to risk losing you again, maybe for good this time. We don't know what we're walking into and I'd just feel better doing a scouting mission first."

"Yes because we have such a great plan... Oh no, wait, we have no plan!"

David grinned at her. "Well we can't really make a solid plan if we don't know anything about the layout, how many people and/or aliens in human skin we are up against, whether they have surveillance or not..."

"So first part of the plan is you and I scope things out."

"Seriously Aggy..."

"I have the gun."

"You could let me have it."

"No, I really couldn't. For one thing you are seriously lacking any sort of actual plan."

"We don't even have any idea what is going on. We might get wherever this truck is going and it isn't the place where they install the presence but just a storage facility. In which case we are going to have to get enough intel..."

"So we're spies now?" David asked with a smile.

"Yes dumbass that's exactly what we are... I'm going with you; my mind is made up."

"Mine too," squawked Doobie from the front seat. "I wanna go, too."

Aggy and David glared at the cage. The parrot was looking back at them through the steel wire bars. If birds could adopt serious expressions Doobie had one. His feathers ruffled. "I wanna go too."

Aggy sneered "Why, so you can rat us out to your friends? I don't think so."

"E.T. phone home! E.T. phone home!" Doobie yelled as he hopped up and down, flapping his wings and getting muffin crumbs all over the van.

"Ignore him," Scooter said.

"If we actually make it in, what are we going to do? What are we really looking for? What if we find the aliens and they have that hateful soul-sucking machine. What then?" David asked.

"I don't think you heard me. I said WE BLOW THEM UP! All of them. And every bit of the soul-extracting technology along with them. These alien bastards are fucking evil!"

"Hey!" Doobie yelled. "Sitting right here... No wait, you're right, we are all evil. That's why we're so afraid of dying."

Aggy gave David a smug look. "You do realize that this

proves what I've always said about religion being the gateway to evil. Even advanced distant alien races have been laid to waste by religion."

"Man, any time you deal with any establishment you got problems that mostly can only be solved by... blowing the fuck out of something!" Scooter said. "Go in, make sure it's the right place, and then boom! It's the only answer."

They were running close enough to the truck that they saw it slow at the end of a long driveway and turn in. Scooter immediately pulled to the side of the road and stopped behind a bunch of bushes which hid them but also obscured their view of the "warehouse." David felt nervous but didn't feel like he was nearly as nervous as he should be. *I think maybe I have entered the numb part of the program. You keep jumping not knowing how deep the water is and eventually you simply stop being worried about what's next because... well you admit you have no idea and it doesn't matter because like it or not you still have to jump.*

The sun was just starting to come up when they all got out of the van and walked over to peer through the hedge. The factory itself looked almost identical to the Weirdough factory he'd worked in.

It was in the middle of nowhere, well off the beaten track. Scooter took a step back then said, "You know why they're here, don't you?"

David looked at him but Aggy just kept looking through the hedge.

"It's the reddest state in the middle of red states. You know what I noticed right after the douche bag won the election? That all the tabloid rags were making him look like the next coming and vilifying anyone who had run against or dared to speak against him. They are published in the south; most of them are sold here. The people who buy and read them believe what's written in them, too. These people are easy to lead around by the nose. All you have to do is claim to be pro-life, pro-guns, anti-gay, and extremely fundamentalist, give them a job and they are just not going to notice anything weird because that's what they do. As long as you say all the things they need you to say for them to trust you they don't give a damn if you're lying."

Aggy turned then to look at him her eyes wide.

"What?" David asked, thinking she had seen something. "He's right," Aggy said. "Scooter is right. Kansas is backwards-thinking enough, but this place... They have purposely put their operations places where no one asks questions as long as you pretend to be just like them. They don't like people who are different. So the aliens just walk in saying and doing what they need to say and do to gain their trust and... It's easy because their human bodies grew up in these places. They know exactly what to say and do to fit in."

Scooter nodded went back to the van and came back with binoculars for everyone and they all went back to peer through the hedge. There were only a handful of security guards and only on the loading dock. If there was another door into the building David wasn't seeing it. There were maybe a dozen cars in the parking lot in total. There was no fence surrounding the property, no guarded gates, and no checkpoints at all. Which would have seemed strange to David before Scooter's revelation.

As they watched, the truck backed up to the loading bay and parked. The driver got out handed a clipboard to a man in a white jump suit then just hung out around the front of the truck. The truck was unloaded by a team of two forklifts in a matter of minutes and then reloaded just as quick. When they realized the truck was about to drive right past them in only a few short minutes they scrambled quickly to load back in the van. Scooter took off and had them well past the entrance when the truck left heading back the way it had come.

Scooter drove a little further down the road then turned onto a dirt road and drove into a small crop of trees that would shelter them from discovery from the road and certainly no one from the factory could see them. They had a mostly-clear view of the factory from where they sat. They got out of the van and started their surveillance again.

Scooter walked to the back of the van and took out a couple of folding chairs. "No sense in being uncomfortable while we save the world."

"Scooter, you are the ultimate 'always be prepared for disaster' Boy Scout." Aggy marveled. Who would have thought that Scooter Stewart The Pot King would be your most valuable player on a mission to destroy an evil alien empire. *I would. Scooter has always been someone I could count on for* *anything... No doubt because I didn't sleep with and have kids with him.*

Scooter pointed a finger at Aggy like a gun, dropped his thumb-trigger, made a "click" noise and in his best John Wayne voice said, "That's Hemp Scout to you, little lady."

"As long as you're grabbing things out of the van I could use something to eat and a coffee," David said.

"Me too," Aggy added.

"Well there's no pizza delivery in the boondocks," Scooter said. "But I do have some MREs and some canned heat."

In minutes Aggy had a warm cup of coffee in her hands. "I will never make fun of the Hemp Scouts again," she swore. Holding her hand up above her head two fingers pinched together as if she was holding a joint.

"Now..." Scooter said solemnly, "swear to uphold the Hemp Scouts honor code. 'I promise not to bogart the joint' and always follow the rule 'Puff, puff, pass'."

He didn't have a pizza MRE, but he did have lasagna which wasn't half bad. The coffee was instant but heated up on the canned heat and sipped from a cup that had been rolling around the floorboards and probably should have been thrown away a couple of days ago... it wasn't half bad... no, it was *all the way* bad, but beggars couldn't be choosers and she wasn't about to complain.

She was drinking the last of the almost coffee and looking through the binoculars when she saw another truck. She quickly jerked the binoculars away from her eyes and yelled out, "I know how to get in!"

CHAPTER FIFTEEN

Mother of a Mother Ship

Aggy never thought in a million years she would be playing this role. *Dear Penthouse, I never thought this could happen to me...* She had dressed as sexy as her luggage would allow and had easily talked the trucker into kinky sex in a no-tell motel room he paid for. He was all over letting her tie him up, but when she opened the door to let David and Scooter in he yelled out, "What the hell! I ain't no queer. I ain't paying for that! Free alright but I ain't paying."

"Scooter don' give nothin' away," Scooter said. He made three snaps in a z pattern in the air.

"Listen here lady, you let me go right now or I'll...."

"Do what exactly?" David hissed. It was sort of cute how mad he was that this guy even thought she was going to give him a little.

The guy opened his mouth to scream and Scooter shut the door behind him. At the same time he said, "You scream and I'll stick something far worse than my dick in your mouth."

"What are you two, her daddy and her grandpa? She came onto me you know."

"We're all the same age you asshole!" Scooter said, obviously taking immediate offense.

David walked over and started going through the guy's pants pockets.

"Oh, I get it," the guy said. "You're just going to roll me for my money... well the joke is on you I ain't got but fifty bucks, and when I tell the cops...."

David pulled the keys out of the guy's pants pockets. "Got them."

"You want my truck... hell, it ain't even mine it belongs to Weirdough, Inc. Go ahead and take it; I don' give a shit."

"Get his ID," Aggy said.

David found the guy's wallet, pulled his ID out of it and threw the wallet down.

"Seriously.... You aren't going to take my money? It's only

fifty bucks but still, what the hell kind of grifters are you?"

"We aren't grifters; we are saving the world from an alien invasion," David said.

David was obviously feeling the need to defend them. Aggy also thought this was cute which meant she was falling back in love with him because thinking annoying things were cute was the first sign.

"Man, I should have known better! My old lady is going to be all... 'I told you to stop fucking lot lizards. I told you I'd put a curse on you...' That fucking witch."

"Shut up," Scooter said. He was acting kind of jumpy which meant the fucker was high. "Man, we need to get out of here before we get caught."

"Fuck this." The guy started to yell, probably for help.

Scooter pulled something from the pocket of his cargo shorts, closed the distance between him and the tied-up trucker in two huge strides then shoved the biggest pot brownie she had ever seen in the man's open mouth. Scooter held his hand over the guy's mouth and held his nose pinched closed.

"Eat the fucking brownie! Eat it!"

The guy choked a couple of times but finally chewed up and swallowed it so that he could breathe again.

Scooter removed his hand.

"Damn man, you didn't lie. I would have rather had your dick in my mouth."

"Don't you make fun of my product!" Scooter yelled. Then he undid the guy's pants and pulled his pants and shorts down around his knees.

"What the fuck man?"

Aggy pointed to the guys tiny wang and laughed.

"Uncool!" The man protested.

David took hold of Scooter's arm in one hand and hers in the other and tugged them out the door slamming it behind them.

"Maybe this wasn't such a good idea," Aggy said. starting to have second thoughts about her own plan. "He's bound to scream and alert the cops and..."

"No guy wants to get caught with his pants around his knees," Scooter assured her. "Besides he just ate two of our super-soakers. They are loaded with enough THC to make an elephant forget. No one's gonna listen to some half-naked, high fucker who's tied to a bed... I should know, I've been there before." Scooter got a misty, faraway look in his eyes. "Ah, good times."

They looked up at the eighteen-wheeler. "Now may seem like a bad time to ask, but does either of you know how to drive one of these things?" Aggy asked.

"I do." Scooter took the keys from Aggy's hand. "Let's make like a baby and go. You two can follow me in the van."

"Do you want the bird so you won't be lonely?" Aggy asked.

"No that's alright." Scooter climbed up into the truck.

Aggy and David went and got in the van, David driving. She was happy when David moved the bird to the back seat and happier still when he thought enough of her to brush the muffin crumbs off the seat.

She climbed in and buckled up. David got in the other side and started the engine just in time to follow Scooter out of the parking lot.

"Any idea where he's going?" she asked.

"Scooter said he saw an old feed store a few miles up the road, looked like it was closed down for good, but the loading dock still looked functional."

Aggy nodded. It was a pretty elaborate plan and those—as far as she was concerned—were always doomed to fail, however she didn't have any better idea.

They drove down the highway for about twenty minutes then Scooter pulled off and drove right down into the loading dock pit, pulled up and then backed down to be unloaded as if he owned the place and was supposed to be there.

David parked the van and then they got out to help Stewart.

There were two dollies in the back of the trailer. While David and Scooter loaded them with crates of the "empty" Weirdough, Aggy kept watch. She didn't really know why. Mostly there were just a few cars running down the highway going both ways and even if cops showed up, or the army or a truck load of alien possessed-humans—short of shooting at them there wasn't much they could do if they got caught. The lock to the interior of the seed storage area was broken, so they opened the door and were just dumping the Weirdough in there in a pile. Aggy was impressed by how fast they were working. In less than a half hour they emptied half the trailer.

"Okay there is plenty of room. Let's put the van in and go," Aggy said, getting more than a little antsy. In truth, the thing she was most worried about was another Weirdough, Inc. truck passing and noticing what they were doing. She wished they were behind the building instead of in front of it, but the loading dock was on the front. When Aggy had asked Scooter why he told her most feed stores were like that because it was easier to get the trucks in and out. It was of course also easier for them to be spotted.

"Hey, big-brained scientist," Scooter said, a hint of laughter in his voice. "I'm pretty sure we can't put the van in the front of the trailer and then put boxes behind it unless we take all the boxes out of the truck."

Aggy felt like beating her head against a wall. He was right of course. She watched as a Weirdough, Inc. truck came into view and her butt clinched a bit. "Man, I see a truck..."

"If they stop tell them the load was shifting and we had to stop and reset it," Scooter said.

Aggy nodded but held her breath as the truck got closer then breathed a sigh of relief as it whizzed right past them.

When the trailer was empty, David got the bird out of the van and Scooter drove the van right up the ramp up onto the loading dock and then he backed it into the trailer. They watched with mild amusement as Scooter then had to get out of the van using techniques normally reserved for contortionists trying to push themselves through a tennis racket.

Scooter got in the sleeper and then she handed him the bird. He didn't complain at all, which told her she was right and Scooter liked the damn thing.

She and David got in the front seat, and now David would be driving. Actually Aggy was surprised David knew how to drive a big rig. After all he was a scientist. As they started down the road it became obvious that he wasn't just saying he could drive the truck, he was actually really good at it.

"Alright I'll admit it, I wasn't sure you could really handle this rig. Where on earth did you learn to drive an 18-wheeler?"

"I didn't graduate at the top of our class like you did, Aggy. I didn't get a job right out of college I spent about six months working at a warehouse. They actually paid me to learn to drive one so that I could back trucks in and out and let's face it that's the hard part. The rest is just driving."

So there was more she didn't know about him than she did, and yet the way she felt about him hadn't really changed at all which... had no scientific basis.

The guard was looking in the back of the truck counting boxes. Another truck was already being unloaded and since there seemed to be only two dock workers unloading and they were doing it with hand trucks it bought them a little time, not a lot but a little.

David handed the guard the trucker's clip board saying, "I'm running a little late. My load shifted and I had to stop and rearrange the boxes."

The guard just nodded and kept counting.

She assumed that he counted the back layer and had some graph somewhere that told him how many boxes were in the truck and then he could check it with the manifest David had handed him.

"I just love traveling with my hubby. It's like a honeymoon that doesn't end," Aggy said as the guard walked away from the back of the truck making a check mark on the paper on the clip board. To David's dismay she kept chattering to him like she was an airhead.

David's guts were churning and his palms were sweaty. *Wow! Aggy's laying it on a little thick! Why doesn't she just wave a giant flag in the air that says, we aren't supposed to be here please kill us.*

The guard handed David's clip board back, a bored expression on his face. "It all looks to be in order."

David leaned over and whispered in Aggy's ear, "That was the worst performance of your life."

"Really? Because it seems to be working," Aggy whispered back. "If we're going to rag on each other's performances dear... You couldn't look guiltier if you were trying on OJ's gloves." She kissed his cheek. "Act, darling, act."

David grinned remembering their drama teacher yelling the same thing at them. Like he had done back then he pulled his act together and remembered to stay in character as he said, "Can we maybe use your restroom..." He tried to look as uncomfortable as possible, and remembering what Scooter had said pulled up a barely-used Southern accent he had laying around. "We were chasing our own ass all the way here. Wasn't much time for stopping after I repacked the load. My old lady needs to take a whiz something awful, and I've had to crap worse but don' remember when."

"Walk in the big door, turn right, keep walking, it's towards the back." The guard waved them on inside.

They walked into the loading area and there were crates of Weirdough everywhere stacked floor to twelve-foot ceiling. To the right and in the back of the warehouse there was a door marked "restroom."

As they walked to it, far out of hearing range of any of the workers, Aggy leaned into him and hissed, "Your old lady! Seriously! I ought to punch you in your testicles!"

"Don't get your panties in a bunch, you told me to act," David whispered back. "I did and, we're in, aren't we?"

They walked to the bathroom opened the door and went inside. It was just a bathroom.

"Hum." Aggy said.

"What?" David asked, walking into one of the stalls because well... he did have to pee.

"I'm a little underwhelmed. I mean shouldn't the lair of evil aliens be... I don't know more evil, not so tidy? Hell, it smells like a Carolina pine forest in here."

"I know," David said, grinning as he shook himself. "Their bathroom is cleaner than your house."

Aggy chuckled. "Hell Scooter's van is cleaner than my house. What's your point?"

"Ah maybe we should focus."

"Why start now? That's just going to muddy the water." He walked out of the stall and Aggy was standing right there waiting for him. "What the hell are we doing really? Seriously if this is where they are loading the alien into the putty, what then? Take pictures, go to the feds? No one's going to believe us. We don't even really know what the hell we're looking for; hell, we may have already seen it."

She had a point.

"Ah..." He walked to the sink and started washing his hands. "I guess we're trying to find out all we can about the enemy. We can't really make any sort of plan till we know... well a hell of a lot more than we do right now."

"Yes, because *we* are *military*." She rolled her eyes. "We aren't even with NASA, David. Hell I mostly work with shit."

He could hear it in her voice. Aggy was nervous, at least as nervous as he was.

"You didn't have to come in. You could have stayed in the truck with Scooter."

"That bird was there," Aggy said with a grin.

"If we find the machine we might be able to destroy it. That would stop them."

"It would probably only slow them down. Well come on let's go if we're going."

David went to the door and peered out. No one was watching and there was a door not six feet away that he was sure lead to the rest of the building.

"If we get caught we just act like we got lost after we used the can."

Aggy nodded and they left the bathroom and made their way to the other door. It wasn't locked and when they walked through it the long hall in front of them looked empty. The wide hall was silent; the only sound was the hissing of air conditioning blowing gently. The exterior wall was nothing unusual, just a flat wall occasionally broken with a window. But the interior wall was smooth and about twelve feet up rounded up and you couldn't see the top of it. As they walked down the hall looking for clues to what was really going on and hoping not to be caught, they realized there were no doors either to the outside or to the interior of the building.

Aggy ran her hand along the wall. "It's cold to the touch and there is a slight vibration."

"A huge vat?" David asked.

Aggy shrugged.

The walls were painted a pale, sterile blue and were perfectly clean. The floors were covered in industrial linoleum, white with grey and blue flecks, that matched the blue of the walls. In fact, the place looked more like a hospital of some sort than a toy-manufacturing plant. There were no chairs so no loitering staff that might stumble on them which was good.

"The design of this building makes no sense. We are walking in a circle basically," Aggy said.

David nodded silently. The longer they went without seeing anyone the surer he was that they were being watched.

They walked for what seemed like a half mile before they finally came to a door in the side of the interior wall. There was a window in the top of it and inside was what was clearly a work area. Peeking in—as covertly as possible —they saw a row of people in disposable blue lab suits wearing face masks, head covers and gloves. The place looked as clean as a surgical suite.

Aggy pointed and David looked to where one person was

busy opening the pre-alien Weirdough containers as a bunch more were taking tubes and fastening them into nipples on the top of what looked like nothing more sophisticated than a series of glass jars. The contents of the glass jars looked like nothing but light. A worker stuck the other end of a tube into one of the Weirdough containers, and soon the light in the jar was gone and the Weirdough was glowing. Then the workers slapped the lid back on the container and packed it.

"They must be packing thousands of them a day," Aggy whispered.

David nodded.

"Come on let's do something highly scientific." She moved quickly away from the door and stuck her ear against the wall.

David nodded and followed suit.

"I am tired of working all the time," one of them said. "If we are to be the rulers of our people why is it that we do nothing but work?"

"We must build an army," another said. "There must be more of us or we will never be able to subjugate the humans."

"I don't give a damn about subjugating humans," still another said. "Let's go to Florida lay on the beach and drink beer."

"Enough of this. Just do the work. When there is an army of us... Then we can go to Florida lay on the beach and drink beer." They all cheered.

At the same time both Aggy and David took their ears away from the wall and looked at each other dumfounded. Then Aggy said, "Doobie is right. They are all assholes."

"Don't tell him; he'll be insufferable."

"And that would be different how?"

They moved to look back through the window. Aggy pointed towards the far wall where there was a small door. Through it he could see a vast cavernous space filled with millions of the jars holding the alien souls.

They looked at each other and whispered together, "It's a ship."

"The middle of the building is a huge, fucking alien ship filled to near breaking with enough alien souls to build that army the assholes were talking about," Aggy whispered.

"I think we know all we need to; let's get the hell out of here," David said.

They started to turn to do just that, but as they did one of the workers turned pointed at them and yelled something. They took off running back the way they had come. David pulled the two-way radio out of his pocket.

"Scooter we've been made. Watch your back."

There was no answer.

"Dammit they must have found Scooter."

Two goons in pin-striped suits no less seemed to appear right in front of them. When they tried to turn to go back the other way two of the blue-garbed masked people they'd been watching were standing behind them.

"Halt!" One of the goons yelled.

They did mostly because there didn't seem to be any real options.

"What are you doing here? This is a restricted zone, very important to maintain sterile conditions at all phases of packing," the same guy said.

He guessed the others weren't big on talking to strangers.

Aggy went into character. "We got lost looking for the bathroom. Too much coffee driving all day and night! You know how that is."

"No... I really have no idea, Dr. Crystal."

"Fucking internet," Aggy muttered for reasons David could only guess at, then she pulled her gun. But as quick as she pulled it out one of those alien soul-sucking bastards kicked it right out of her hand like he was a ninja.

David should have known better, but out of options he punched one of them. Too bad the body the thing wore was three times David's size. He dropped David with one punch.

Aggy immediately dropped beside him and whispered, "Pretend you're hurt worse than you are."

David was pretty sure she had no idea how bad he was hurt.

Aggy could tell David wasn't out, but he sure as hell wasn't a hundred percent which was probably for the best because they were no doubt about to be killed in a really horrible way.

That being the case, ignoring the aliens that surrounded her she blurted out, "David... I have always loved you."

"I love you too, Aggy."

There was a load noise and then Aggy was covered in gooey body junk and blood. "Less kissing more running!" Scooter's voice called out.

"Am I ever glad to see you..." Aggy started.

"Hold that thought, Aggy," Scooter said, throwing the strap of the howitzer he was holding over his shoulder and running over to help her pick David up. "We have about five minutes before this whole place blows up."

They ran down the hall and onto the loading bay where there was no one in sight. In answer to Aggy's unasked question Scooter yelled out, "You would be surprised how fast people move when you tell them the building they are in is about to blow up. God bless Homeland Security and their constant red and orange warnings!"

"And I never thought there would be anything good that could come of the Trump presidency," Aggy mumbled.

Scooter had already pulled the van out of the truck, so she and Scooter put David in the back seat. Aggy got in, slammed the door, then moved to mostly hold David up. Scooter jumped into the driver's seat slammed the door and took off. At the end of the driveway Scooter turned the van around.

"Burn Baby burn!" Scooter yelled at the building. There was a loud, ear-ringing boom and then the whole building blew up as Scooter had promised.

"Quit gloating and get moving," Aggy ordered. "There was a space ship in there. No idea what the propulsion unit was, but we can't rule out nuclear."

Scooter spun the van back around and took off back the way they had come. There was a second explosion worse than the first, and the van rocked so violently that Scooter could barely keep them on the road.

In his cage, Dobbie swung back and forth yelling, "Fry you fuckers, fry! I never liked any of you assholes anyway. More Earth for me!" He turned his little birdie head and looked at Scooter. "Well that's one."

"That's one?" Scooter screeched.

"There are at least a half a dozen ships. There were a lot of assholes on our planet, lots more than one ship full."

CHAPTER SIXTEEN

Bring in the Clowns

Scooter pulled into Aggy's driveway and stopped. David opened the door and got out taking his luggage with him. Aggy climbed out after him carrying hers. Scooter opened the back doors.

"You know what, Scooter?" Aggy said, a weary tone to her voice. "Just leave the rest of my crap in the van. I don't need any of it right this minute. You can bring it by the lab after the holidays."

Scooter nodded and closed the doors. "We'll have to figure out what we do next anyway," Scooter said. Because of course on their way home the news had broken about the Weirdough, Inc. warehouse blowing up and...

Well no one was saying anything about the remains of a huge, alien space craft, so the government was covering it up faster than a cat covered its crap when it shit in the flower bed. Scooter said he didn't trust the government and Aggy agreed saying they were more likely to get disappeared by the government than they were the aliens.

David wanted to disagree with them. He would have liked nothing better than to tell the government what they knew and leave it for them to handle, but under the current administration he couldn't really make an argument that the government could be trusted with anything much less this.

Aggy walked over and hugged Scooter. "Thanks, Scooter for saving our lives and everything else."

When Aggy and Scooter had hugged a lot longer than David thought was necessary, David hugged Scooter's neck and said, "Yes Scooter thanks for everything."

"I love you guys." Scooter sniffled and let David go only after nearly crushing his rib cage. "I've got to go; whole family and all my employees are losing their shit. Believe it or not the whole lot of them seem to be incapable of anything without my constant help."

"Actually," David grinned. "I have no problem at all believing that."

"You guys have a great holiday. Relax and enjoy each other. Don't worry; there may be more of them out there but we'll find them and at least for now we've stopped them."

They followed Scooter to his door and watched as he opened it and got in. "Be careful, Scooter, they may be watching us, especially you."

Scooter laughed. "They won't find much of interest. Let them watch. Hell I've been mostly looking over my shoulder my whole life."

"Don't worry," Doobie said. "They are all a bunch of chicken shit assholes. You blew one of the ships up. They aren't going to want to mess with you. As a species we lack anything approaching actual courage. You know like David..."

"Why you little green piece of shit I ought to..."

"And that's why I'm taking him with me; consider it a special holiday present. You guys be careful and play nice." He grinned at them and then shut the door. They watched him back out of the drive way and then continued to watch him till he was out of sight.

They both sighed turned and started for the front door only to find that it had been jimmied open. Aggy dropped her bag and grabbed her gun. They walked in.

"They've tossed the place," Aggy whispered.

"How can you tell?" David asked. It didn't look any different to him. David followed her from room to room as she checked to make sure the perps weren't there waiting for them which they weren't. Aggy put her gun back in its holster.

"I'm sorry, Aggy. That was a stupid, insensitive joke. They know you're involved; that's not funny. And I know how you must feel because I know how I felt when they trashed my house..."

"Chill out, David." Aggy smiled and patted his cheek. "You're right. They haven't made a much bigger mess than it was and my TV, stereo and computer are missing so it wasn't the aliens. I've actually been robbed. If I'm sad at all it's because now I know the cat is dead." He gave her a curious look and she shrugged. "For reasons known only to the hoods that robbed my house they moved the washer and there were the desiccated remains of my cat where the guys who delivered my washer apparently didn't see him and crushed him. At least he went quickly..."

"How do you know that?" David asked.

"Seriously, David, if that thing had been alive it would have been screaming bloody murder and surely they wouldn't have just left him here.... Though now it makes sense that they said they had a lot of trouble leveling it."

David's face must have shown what he was thinking because she asked, "What's wrong?"

"Aren't you the least bit upset someone broke into your house and stole your stuff?"

"I don't own any valuable jewelry. I don't keep money in the house. I needed a new TV and stereo anyway, and I haven't used my home computer since I got the lap top I had before this one. They could have just trashed the place out they didn't. I can bury my cat, order a pizza and use my own bathroom. There are aliens on our planet. We are fighting them on our own with our good friend the stoner, and our whole plan to stop them even for the moment hinges on the world's most obnoxious clown. Nothing is the same as it was before you showed up in my lab and... How do I say this without sounding crazy... I'm glad."

She walked up to him and wrapped her arms around his neck and he kissed her. She kissed him right back then looked up at him and said, "I always wanted to do something important and now I have and will continue to. I missed you; I didn't know how much."

"And I always missed you and always knew just how much. I hate to say it, but creepy aliens living in a children's toy aside, this has been one of the greatest times of my life. I had just been going through the motions for years. I wasn't living I was just existing. Whatever happens I'm never going to do that again, Aggy. So... can I stay?"

Because of course when Scooter had said he really needed to get home and it was quicker to get back to Colorado Springs if they took a more direct route that didn't go through the KC area, David was all over taking the quicker route because it gave him an excuse to stay closer to Aggy at least a little while longer.

"Oh... you're staying. You don't get to drag me into all this crap and then just go."

He bent down and kissed her again. "You order a pizza and I'll bury the cat."

They had spoken with Pork Chop on the phone a half a dozen times and each time he assured them he had everything under control, yet for some reason they just didn't trust that he really did.

It was Christmas morning. Aggy didn't believe in baby Jesus but she used to like the holiday and this was the first time in years that she was spending it with anyone at all. She got up before David and walked into her kitchen, determined to use it for the first time in years. The robbery had given them an excuse to clean the place and they'd done it together. She didn't report the robbery; they literally hadn't taken anything but the TV, stereo and computer—none of which were worth sending a junkie to jail over. She and David went and bought a new entertainment system as a holiday gift for themselves.

She was in the middle of making sausage and pancakes when David walked in. He sniffed deeply then true to his smart-ass roots said, "That doesn't smell like pizza."

"I could fix that by sticking a little oregano in the batter," Aggy said, not turning to look at him because she was busy trying not to burn food.

David walked up behind her and wrapped his arms around her waist.

"A new Christmas tradition? Pizza cakes. Ahh this smells pretty good just like it is." He let her go and moved to lean against the sink so he could look at her. "Nervous?"

Aggy nodded. They had changed so much as people and yet in so many ways it was like they'd never been apart. They were learning new things about each other yet she still knew him in a way she hadn't ever known anyone else. "I'd be less nervous if the fate of the free world didn't rest on Pork Chop the clown."

"Yep exactly how I felt election night except I think Pork Chop has the world's best interest at heart."

They ate breakfast then went to the living room and spent several minutes trying to figure out just how to turn the new TV on. Each of them sure the other one wasn't doing it right till they switched who was trying three times and finally figured it out together. It was hours away, so they watched some Christmas movie and cuddled on the couch trying not to think about what they were going to do if the commercial aired as planned.

It was one straight up and there he was, Pork Chop the Weirdough clown. Aggy was sure neither she nor David was breathing. Here it was, the moment of truth, if Pork Chop had failed they wouldn't have a few dozen kids to find and scare the alien out of them, there would be millions. An unstoppable army and maybe, just maybe, they shouldn't have left the fate of humanity in the hands of a chain-smoking, booze-guzzling clown. In retrospect it seemed like that was the worst part of their plan.

"Hey, hey boys and girls! Merry Christmas from everyone at Weirdough, Inc., and me, Pork Chop! Now it's time for the best Weirdough trick of all. Everyone get your Weirdough containers. Make sure all your brothers and sisters and friends are watching; we don't want anyone to feel left out. After all no one likes to feel left out...."

"I don't know, David..."

"Shush."

Aggy's stomach was turning a little and it wasn't just because of the clown.

...Are you all ready?" Pork Chop asked. "Be very careful when you open your Weirdough container that you do not touch it at all or the trick will not work. Go to a window—any window or door in your house—and dump the Weirdough out of its container onto the ground. Don't touch it; leave it where it falls then close the window or door and walk away. In a few hours go back to where you dumped it and you will get a huge surprise."

Beside her Aggy heard David start to breathe again and so did she. They looked at each other then jumped up and started dancing around. "Never thought I'd say this, but I love that fucking clown."

"Amen!" David said.

The phone rang and David answered it.

"Yeah we saw it, Scooter... Yes you did say he would come through... Where did you put him up?" Because of course Pork Chop had gone into hiding as soon as he was sure he had successfully swapped the commercial out and destroyed the original. "Hollywood?... Well tell him we wish him all the luck in the world... Merry Christmas to you too, Scooter, and for the record you're our hero." David hung the phone up with a chuckle.

"What is Pork Chop doing in Hollywood?" Aggy asked.

"Since he can't play Pork Chop anymore he has decided to try his hand at dramatic acting," David said. "Scooter gave him enough cash that he can afford to at least give it a try."

"You know I've seen stranger things," Aggy said. "That clown deserves a medal. I hope he gets to do exactly what he wants to do. Right now instead of millions of children being taken over by aliens, millions of aliens are sitting in the dirt or the snow dying. Hell we all deserve medals."

David grabbed her and held her. "And God bless us all, everyone."

ABOUT SELINA ROSEN

Selina Rosen is the author of over twenty-five novels including *Sword Masters* and *Strange Robby*, and she has had dozens of short stories published in professional venues including *Thieves World* and *Impossible Monsters*. As editor-in-chief of Yard Dog Press she has edited ten anthologies including *Bubbas of the Apocalypse*. She is married, owns a small farm, and has kids and grandkids. She is a carpenter, a rock mason, a sword fighter and an all-around swell gal.

Selina says, "I started writing at twelve as an escape. The situations I have lived through are the stuff of which my fiction is born. My relationships with the many and varied people I have come into contact with over the years is a catalogue of characters from which I pull."

Selina and her wife of nearly twenty-six years own a small farm where Selina raises milk goats, rabbits, chickens and a garden. She raises—depending on the weather and bugs—between forty and sixty percent of their food mostly organically. (By "mostly" she means if it looks like she'll lose an animal she will do what she thinks is necessary.) They make no trash: using, repurposing, or recycling everything.

Selina fought heavy weapons (and trained other fighters) with the SCA for about twelve years, but was talked into fencing many years ago. Though she sold all her armor and heavy weapons she still fences. She has also now been doing do a mixture of Tai Chi and Chi Gung every day for the last five years.

"Anyone who reads my work knows more about the real me than I could ever put in a bio. If you want to talk to me, find me on Facebook. If you see me somewhere, come right up and talk to me. I am just like you. Luckily, I have a job I love, and the reason I have this great job is that people like you let me."—Selina

ABOUT SHERRI DEAN

Sherri Dean was born late AND backwards in a small town in Missouri, which explains a lot. In the past she spent many years of her mundane hours as a veteran of the animal health field (and the recipient of many a puppy piddling) but is presently on hiatus as she perfects the art of becoming rich and famous. Or was that infamous? She spends her quality time writing, illustrating, making crazy costumes and reading.

She credits Forrest J "Uncle Forry" Ackerman for her love of Science Fiction, fantasy and horror, and is active in genre conventions throughout the Midwest. It is at one of these early conventions she encountered the infamous (there's that word again! Buy a thesaurus already!) Selina "BUY MY BOOKS!" Rosen and was thusly corrupted to submit cover art, stories and mad editing skills for Yard Dog Press. Among Sherri's available works are the Weird Western collection with co-author Bill D. Allen titled *Three Aces From Satan's Hand* and the horror anthology *Death is Only Skin Deep* with Tim W. Burke and Allison Stein. Both are available online, so get crackin' as they won't last long!

Sherri has long referred to herself in the third person, the "royal we," if you will, as the Queen of the Flying Monkeys for years and has recently earned the title of The Feisty Mistress of Fear. (If you've met her you already know. If not, do so and BUY HER STUFF!) In addition to commanding her monkey minions she likes shiny presents and hearing from fans on Facebook, Twitter and the upcoming website. Now, go forth and make with the monkey adoration! She needs praise; lie if you must.

ABOUT BRAD FOSTER THE COVER ARTIST

Brad W. Foster is an award-winning artist who has had work published in over a thousand books, magazines, comics, and indefinable small press publications—the man needs a hobby!

Brad has created several covers for Yard Dog Press, including *Illusions of Sanity, Hammer Town, Dadgum Martians Invade the Lucky Nickel Saloon, Fairy BrewHaHa at the Lucky Nickel Saloon, Jaguar Moon,* and *Bride of Tranquility.*

Brad draws to live and finds it interesting that he also lives to draw. You can find out even more about Brad and his work at: http://www.jabberwockygraphix.com.

Yard Dog Press Titles As Of This Print Date

A Bubba in Time Saves None, Edited by Selina Rosen
A Man, A Plan, (yet lacking) A Canal, Panama, Linda Donahue
Adventures of the Irish Ninja, Selina Rosen
The Alamo and Zombies, Jean Stuntz
All the Marbles, Dusty Rainbolt
Almost Human, Gary Moreau
Ancient Enemy, Lee Killouth
*The Anthology From Hell: Humorous Tales From WAY Down
     Under,* Edited by Julia S. Mandala
Ard Magister, Laura J. Underwood
Assassins Inc., Phillip Drayer Duncan
Bad City, Selina Rosen & Laura J. Underwood
Bad Lands, Selina Rosen & Laura J. Underwood
Black Rage, Selina Rosen
Blackrose Avenue, Mark Shepherd
The Boat Man, Selina Rosen
Bobby's Troll, John Lance
Bride of Tranquility, Tracy S. Morris
Bruce and Roxanne from Start to Finnish, Rie Sheridan Rose
The Bubba Chronicles, Selina Rosen
Bubba Fables, Sue P. Sinor
Bubbas Of the Apocalypse, Edited by Selina Rosen
The Burden of the Crown, Selina Rosen
Chains of Redemption, Selina Rosen
Checking On Culture, Lee Killough
Chronicles of the Last War, Laura J. Underwood
Dadgum Martians Invade the Lucky Nickel Saloon, Ken Rand
Dark and Stormy Nights, Bradley H. Sinor
Deja Doo, Edited by Selina Rosen
Dracula's Lawyer, Julia S. Mandala
Dragon's Tongue, Laura J. Underwood
The Essence of Stone, Beverly A. Hale
Fairy BrewHaHa at the Lucky Nickel Saloon, Ken Rand
The Fantastikon: Tales of Wonder, Robin Wayne Bailey
Fire & Ice, Selina Rosen
Flush Fiction, Volume I: Stories To Be Read In One Sitting, Edited
     by Selina Rosen
Flush Fiction, Volume II: Twenty Years of Letting it Go!, Edited by
     Selina Rosen
*The Four Bubbas of the Apocalypse: Flatulence, Halitosis, Incest,
     and... Ned,* Edited by Selina Rosen
The Four Redheads: Apocalypse Now!, Linda L. Donahue,
     Rhonda Eudaly, Julia S. Mandala, & Dusty Rainbolt
The Four Redheads of the Apocalypse, Linda L. Donahue,
     Rhonda Eudaly, Julia S. Mandala, & Dusty Rainbolt
The Four Redheads: The Wrath of Satan, Linda L. Donahue,

Fantasy Writers Asylum (A YDP Imprint):

Blood Songs
Julia Mandala
Gateway to Corimar
Julia Mandala & Linda L Donahue
Tale of the Black Heart
Linda L. Donahue

Non-YDP titles we distribute:

Chains of Freedom
Chains of Destruction
Jabone's Sword
Queen of Denial
Recycled
Strange Robby
Sword Masters
Selina Rosen

Three Ways to Order:

1. Write us a letter telling us what you want, then send it along with your check or money order (made payable to Yard Dog Press) to: Yard Dog Press, 710 W. Redbud Lane, Alma, AR 72921-7247

2. Use selinarosen@cox.net or lynnstran@cox.net to contact us and place your order. Then send your check or money order to the address above. *This has the advantage of allowing you to check on the availability of short-stock items such as T-shirts and back-issues of Yard Dog Comics.*

3. Contact us as in #1 or #2 above and pay with a credit card or by debit from your checking account. Either give us the credit card information in your letter/Email/phone call, or go to our website and use our shopping carts. If you send us your information, please include your name as it appears on the card, your credit card number, the expiration date, and the 3 or 4-digit security code after your signature on the back (CVV). Please remember that we will include media rate (minimum $3.00) S/H for mailing in the lower 48 states.

*Watch our website at
www.yarddogpress.com
for news of upcoming projects
and new titles!!*

A Note to Our Readers

We at Yard Dog Press understand that many people buy used books because they simply can't afford new ones. That said, and understanding that not everyone is made of money, we'd like you to know something that you may not have realized. Writers only make money on new books that sell. At the big houses a writer's entire future can hinge on the number of books they sell. While this isn't the case at Yard Dog Press, the honest truth is that when you sell or trade your book or let many people read it, the writer and the publishing house aren't making any money.

As much as we'd all like to believe that we can exist on love and sweet potato pie, the truth is we all need money to buy the things essential to our daily lives. Writers and publishers are no different.

We realize that these "freebies" and cheap books often turn people on to new writers and books that they wouldn't otherwise read. However we hope that you will reconsider selling your copy, and that if you trade it or let your friends borrow it, you also pass on the information that if they really like the author's work they should consider buying one of their books at full price sometime so that the writer can afford to continue to write work that entertains you.

We appreciate all our readers and *depend* upon their support.

Thanks,
The Editorial Staff
Yard Dog Press

PS – Please note that "used" books without covers have, in most cases, been stolen. Neither the author nor the publisher has made any money on these books because they were supposed to be pulped for lack of sales.

Please do not purchase books without covers.